Solution
Committee

Solution Committee

Jon Grimm

ISBN-13: 9780578164458
ISBN-10: 0578164450

Library of Congress Control Number: 2016904528
John Grimaldi, Zellwood, FL

To my wife, Christine, without whose help and inspiration this book would not have been completed

CHAPTER 1

THE PARTY

What makes a party really great? Of course, great food, lively music, stimulating conversation and beautiful people just added to the party atmosphere. The stunning twenty-five-thousand-square-foot stone mansion on a hundred acres of Virginia countryside was the perfect setting.

Upon driving through the huge wrought-iron gates supported by stone pillars, guests were taken aback by the beautiful rolling green pastures, grazing horses, and miles of white split-rail fencing. As the long, winding road turned to the left, a huge circular driveway came into view with the old-world-style estate in the background.

The valets immediately greeted the arriving guests and parked their vehicles.

This grand country estate belonged to Jameson Burns, the heir to the Burns Construction company fortune. Burns often threw lavish parties for the charities he supported. This, a National Cancer Society fundraiser, was an annual event and was well known as Burns' favorite.

Samuel Webster (D-California) had been in the Senate for thirty years and was the chairman of the Senate Intelligence Committee. He and his wife, Elizabeth, enjoyed attending Mr. Burns' parties, which were always extravagant affairs. They liked catching up with old friends and meeting new ones, and, of course, being seen at these charity events didn't hurt the senator's image.

Elizabeth had to attend another event and could not be at the party with Sam tonight. Although he missed her, he was enjoying himself this evening. Sam was always a hit at these affairs. Everyone wanted to speak with the popular Democratic senator. He loved these conversations with his constituents—personal contact meant votes.

"Hi, Senator," came a voice from the crowd. "Anything new happening in the spy business?" It was Dr. Robert Smith, the senator's personal physician and good friend. They were golf buddies and regularly played together. Their wives were good friends and the two couples often went out to dinner together.

"How would I know? I'm just a senator," said Sam. They all laughed. Denise, the doctor's wife, joined the group, took Sam's hand, and swept him onto the dance floor. Sam enjoyed dancing with Denise.

When they finished their dance, Sam and Denise returned to the doctor and the group of friends surrounding him. Others joined the conversation. Someone in the crowd asked about the senator's Health Care for New Immigrants bill. "It's coming up for a vote in the next couple of weeks, I think," said Sam.

The partying continued, and as the night progressed, Sam felt a tap on his shoulder and turned to see a beautiful woman with Asian features. She was tall and slim with long, silky black hair. The form-fitting, one-shoulder black dress fit her body to perfection. *All right*, he thought, *this is my kind of voter.*

Before he could speak, she said, "Senator, would you like to dance?" The next thing he knew; he was in her arms. *Nice fit*, the California senator thought as she cuddled really close. *This could be a fun night.* When the dance ended, she whispered into his ear, "nice meeting you, Senator. Good luck with your bill." She then turned and disappeared into the crowd.

That was a nice surprise. Too bad I didn't get a chance to show her my limousine, he thought as he headed toward the bar for one last drink. Again, his friends gathered around him. There were a couple of smirks and wisecracks about his hot dancing partner.

"Don't worry," Doc laughed. "I won't tell Elizabeth about your new friend."

It was getting late, and the senator was tired. He looked at his watch. It was past midnight, and the party was winding down. It had been a long day. As he walked through the crowd and said his good nights, he called for his car to take him home.

Sam got into the back seat and closed his eyes. He thought back to the party. *He'd danced, drank, had some stimulating conversations, and met some interesting people. It had been a good night.*

When Sam arrived home, he felt a nervous chill run through his body. He didn't think much about it, just continued getting undressed and fell into bed. The pillowcase felt cool on his neck, and he breathed deeply. It felt good.

Elizabeth was not home yet. *He wondered if her event was successful and if she would have any gossip to share with him.* Sam closed his eyes.

A couple of days later, the lead story in the *Washington Post* read, Senator Samuel Webster (D-California), the four-term chairman of the Senate Intelligence Committee, passed away this weekend.

He had an apparent heart attack at his
DC home on Sunday morning.

When his wife could not wake him, she dialed
911. By the time the paramedics arrived at the
home, he was not breathing. Senator Sam
Webster was pronounced dead at the hospital.
His Health Care for Illegal Immigrants Bill,
S-2673, was dead as well.

CHAPTER 2

CARRYING THE BALL

Representative Marline Dewhurst (D-Oregon) held a very progressive outlook on America. She had been a congresswoman for five terms—ten years now. On this beautiful fall morning in the nation's Capitol, she was enjoying her coffee on the secluded patio of her Georgetown condo and reading the *Washington Post*. The first thing she read was the disturbing article on the death of her friend, Senator Samuel Webster.

The senator was getting ready to go to committee with his controversial Health Care for Illegal Immigrants Bill, S-2673. This bill would add ten million more people to the President's health care bill and bring the total to about forty-five million beneficiaries. The word we get now is that the bill may never get to a vote.

Oh my God, I didn't know Sam had heart trouble, I have to call Elizabeth Representative Dewhurst thought. It was Senator Webster who had convinced her to run for office twelve years ago.

Marline and the senator's wife, Elizabeth, had gone to Stanford University together. They had remained good friends over the years and since they now both lived in the DC area, saw each other often.

Her mind wandered back to their college days, to the time when the two had gone backpacking through Europe. *They'd flown into Rome, had driven from there to St. Tropez in the south of France, and had finally ended up in Paris! They were two twenty-year-olds in the city of love. That really was a fun and exciting time!* Getting back to reality, Marline knew how much her friend must be hurting and how much she needed to be there for her.

Marline picked up the phone to call Elizabeth, but the line was busy. She hung up. After trying several more times to get through to her friend, she gave up, got dressed, and headed to the Webster home.

Marline spent the afternoon comforting and helping her friend through this difficult time. They cried together and laughed together and talked about old times. Elizabeth spoke about Sam's political career. "He worked a lot. When he wasn't doing that, he was playing golf." They had been together a long time. She couldn't imagine life without him.

Marline asked about his senate business. "How were things going?"

"I don't know," Elizabeth responded. "He never talked about his work. I could tell when he had a bad day, he was grumpy. I would ask him about it, but he said not to worry. He laughed when he told me about how he was able to control most of his cohorts. He said it had taken him a long time to be in that position and took all the advantage that he could."

"Do you know what he was talking about?" Marline asked.

"Not really. Sam was very strong willed, though I think he had something on all of them and they voted his way or else."

"I wonder what it was," Marline said.

"I know he really wanted this bill to pass," Elizabeth said. He was pulling out all the stops."

Congresswoman Dewhurst was a strong liberal voice in the House. She decided she was going to push the bill for Sam. *It is a good bill, and I am going to try to co-sponsor it. I'll just make a big enough fuss to get these old boys to listen*, she thought.

CHAPTER 3

THE FUNERAL

It was a cool, clear fall day in Washington, DC. The funeral for Senator Samuel Webster, at St. John's Episcopal Church on Lafayette Square, was packed. The bishop, who knew Sam personally, presided over the service. He spoke of his friendship with the senator and reminisced about the many years they had known each other.

Although it was solemn service, it was also a social gathering Everyone was there: senators, congressmen, cabinet members, and the Vice President of the United States. Webster had earned respect during his long tenure in the Senate. He was known for getting things done and was liked by many of his colleagues and party members for his tenacity.

Condolences were offered to Elizabeth and the family—their three daughters and four grandchildren. Everyone expressed how much he would be missed. Sam Webster had been a loyal Democrat and worked with many on both sides of the aisle.

After graduating from the University of Southern California, Sam decided Washington would offer him the best opportunities to meet the influential people who could help his career and provide him with the lifestyle he envisioned. He landed a job as a law clerk in a prestigious DC firm.

As Elizabeth sat at the funeral, she thought back to when she and Sam had first met. *Sam had been working for a prominent law firm in DC when he was first introduced to Congressman Harold Clark (D-California), Elizabeth's father. Clark took an immediate liking to the young and ambitious attorney. When the congressman offered Sam a job as an assistant aide, Sam was thrilled. That was the beginning of his long and successful career in politics.*

Congressman and Mrs. Clark always hosted their annual St. Jude's Children's Hospital fundraiser on their large California estate. In 1973 it was being held on a perfect afternoon in early September. Sam, the new aide and Elizabeth, the congressman's youngest daughter, had been introduced by her father. After chatting for several hours, they'd realized how much they had in common. They started dating with the congressman's blessings, had fallen in love quickly and were married a year later. They had been together ever since.

There were old faces at the funeral that Elizabeth hadn't seen in a very long time. Many came up to the family and offered their condolences. She'd also noticed some ignored her and didn't even come to pay their respect to her. They stayed back and talked among themselves. *I guess being seen is what was important. She wondered about that and the few snide remarks she overheard. But how sincere were they? I guess one can't be in congress as long as Sam was and not make a few enemies.*

After the funeral, the congressional members returned to their offices and quickly got back to "business as usual". Most were preoccupied with their concerns about who was going to replace the senator and what effect his death would have on them and the party. Governor Robert Arnold, a Republican, would be making that decision.

The Senator had been near the end of his fifth term and since there was less than a year until the next election, the governor would probably make this important appointment instead of calling for an election to choose a new senator. The latter was an expensive proposition, and the money would have to come from the state's budget. The governor would more than likely appoint a Republican to replace the Democrat Senator, Sam Webster.

CHAPTER 4

GOOD-OLD-BOY NETWORK

Senator Will Thomason (R), the junior senator from Florida, walked into Senator Vern Holloway's (D-Maine) office. "Is he in?" Will asked the senator's aide, Julie Madison. Julie, a very attractive blonde in her early fifties, was a widow. She had been with Senator Holloway for twenty years, and rumors had been going around for a long time that she and the senator were romantically involved. As with most rumors, no one knew if they were true.

"Yes, he is," she responded. "I'll let him know you're here." She disappeared into the Senator's office, returning a few minutes later. "Go right in, Senator."

As Will entered the Senator's private office, Holloway said, "Good to see you, Will." He stood and offered his hand. "And you too, Senator Holloway," Will said as they shook hands.

This office is beautiful, Will thought. The wood trim must have been from the early eighteen nineties along with some of the decorative furnishings. The walls were lined with pictures of Holloway shaking hands with several past presidents as well as some very famous people. Will sat in the overstuffed armchair in front of the vast desk and nervously played with the small marble sculpture on the table beside him.

"So what's up?" Senator Holloway asked.

"I'd like to speak with you about the Surveillance Camera Bill, S-2784."

"There is nothing to discuss, Will," Holloway replied. "If you look at the laws, people traveling in automobiles on public thoroughfares have no reasonable expectation of privacy in their movements from one place to another."

"I understand that, Senator, but there are criminal abuses to consider. There was a case in 1999, right here in DC, where a policeman was caught scanning license plate numbers in parking lots to gather information on patrons of a gay club. He was looking up the plate numbers of cars parked at the club, researching the backgrounds of the vehicles' owners, and then trying to blackmail the married ones. Imagine what someone like that could do with a citywide spy-camera system."

"We can control that," Senator Holloway replied. "We have to be vigilant and set up road blocks so the bad guys will be deterred. This bill outweighs your concerns about the very small minority who may be affected in an instance like that. I've given this a lot of thought, Will. I am bringing it to committee next week and then to the floor for a vote. The Senate's locked up. I am working on the House. It's pretty close—"

"But Senator," Will interrupted, "this bill is not good for the country. It's unconstitutional. There will be lawsuits galore if this is passed."

Holloway responded, "It doesn't matter. By the time it's passed, most people won't care about it. Besides, I'm pretty sure the Supreme Court will go along with it. Back off, Will. You can't win this fight," he said as he pounded his fist once on his desk and then continued. "Do yourself a favor: side with me on this one, and I will help get all your bills through the Senate."

At that moment, the phone rang. The Senator looked at the number, turned to Will and said dismissively, "I have to take this call. Don't worry, and don't vote against me. I never forget!"

Will rose and left the senior senator's office. He felt nothing but contempt for this guy wanted to punch him in the mouth, but of course he didn't. As a freshman senator, Will needed to learn the ropes. He'd often heard about the "good-old-boys network," and now he was getting to see how it worked—up close and personal.

CHAPTER 5

THE SYSTEM

O n the walk back to his office, Will began thinking about these senior senators and how they'd just about controlled the Senate. *They had been in office for way too long. They'd built up too many favors and had too much power. It would be almost impossible to vote them out. That is one of the main problems with our government.* He'd wondered *whatever happened to term limits. The US Marine Corps had ways to get things done. But that's the military; this is the Senate!*

He'd remembered back to his time in Iraq. *When his squad entered a village being controlled by a strong warlord. He had already reached the rank of Captain, had completed two tours and had learned to speak their language. The large village was made up of at least one thousand men, women, and children who were being abused by this thug. Captain Thomason had tried to reason with this warlord, but to no avail. A gun fight ensued, and the leader was killed.*

Afterward, Will had spoken with the village people about electing a new leader from among their ranks. He explained how it worked. They listened to what he said and after many questions and discussions among themselves, followed his advice. That was their first taste of democracy. He felt like he'd made a difference and he'd liked the results.

There had been a lot of controversy over the new bill Senator Vern Holloway was trying to get to committee. It would affect millions of people. The senior Democrat was one of the most liberal members of the Senate. Holloway's new bill, S-2784 (the Save America Crime Bill), would put surveillance cameras with facial recognition capabilities on every street in America. Many saw this as a Fourth Amendment violation. Under most circumstances, no one would be worried that a bill like this would ever get out of committee, let alone to the floor. However, after twenty-five years in the Senate, Senator Vern Holloway was owed a lot of favors. The senator knew the president would sign the bill. After all, he'd helped President Hutton get elected. That made this bill very scary to Will as well as many conservative senators. They were mounting a fight to stop it.

CHAPTER 6

THE NEW SENATOR

Will was getting angrier and angrier as he approached his office. He opened the door and all hell was breaking loose. All the phones were ringing at once. His secretary, Margaret, had ten messages for him. His aide, Christie, was waiting to speak with him. There were two constituents from Florida waiting to see him with their problems. And, most important of all, he had to pee. Even with all this chaos surrounding him, Will could not stop thinking about Holloway's Save America Crime Bill. He greeted everyone and headed into his private office.

The masculine-looking office was small. It had dark wooden wainscoting, dark-green carpet, a burgundy leather sofa, and two green leather chairs. The cream-colored walls were covered with many photographs. Some were from Will's marine days, with group settings in Iraq. Another photo showed him with the US ambassador to Israel; it was taken when he was part of the US mission in Tel Aviv. There were other photos from his visit to Germany, as well as a copy of his degree from the University of Florida in Gainesville and his separation papers from active duty on the wall next to the door.

His aide, Christie Adams, followed him into his office and closed the door behind her. "Senator, we have a lot to talk about. You have a vote in forty-five minutes and three important phone calls you need to return right away."

He walked into the bathroom and closed the door on Christie, hoping she wouldn't follow him in there, too! Pee and think—what a concept!

Will Thomason had been a senator for almost two years now. In his military days he had been one tough and smart jarhead. .He thought back to his time in marine recon. He had served his country for more than thirteen years and had entertained the idea of making the military his career.

One day, at the age of thirty-five, after an extremely restless night, he'd awakened to the realization that time had been passing him by and he needed to analyze his future. *Did he really want to be a marine for the rest of his life? Was it enough?* He'd weighed the pros and cons and had done much soul-searching over the next few days. Finally, he had come to the conclusion that he just might be happier doing something more with his life. He was not sure what that *more* would be, but he knew he needed to explore other avenues.

Will was a native Floridian who grew up in Orlando in an upper-middle-class community. His father, William Thomason III, was an engineer and his mother, Mary, was an artist. As a handsome bachelor in his mid-thirties, he had a strong personality and quick wit. He stood six feet two inches and weighed 225 pounds—all muscle. He ran about five miles a day and worked out regularly at the gym. With his rugged good looks, dark hair, and brown eyes, he was considered "hot" by many women.

On a rainy afternoon in April, when Will had been home on leave, he had been drinking a cup of coffee and reading the newspaper when he'd seen the headline in the *Orlando Sentinel*: "Senator Joseph Harding is dead from an apparent heart attack, leaving a vacancy in the Florida Senate."

Senator Harding had just been reelected for a second term at the time of his death. Will was reasoning, *with most of the six-year Senate term still unfilled, the governor of Florida would probably order a special election for a new senator.*

At that moment, phone rang. It was his best friend, Zack Miller. After a friendly conversation, the discussion turned to the article Will had just read regarding Senator Harding's death.

Zack said to Will, "You're looking for a new direction; why don't you consider politics? Since I'm already living and working in

DC, I might be able to help. And, besides, it would be great to live in the same city again."

He'd thought Zack was crazy at first. "I have no experience. I've never run for any office."

"So what?" Zack said. "You're a lot better than most of the people who are there now. You're a take-charge guy and would not be afraid to fight for what you think is right."

As Will had thought about it, he'd realized Zack might be right. *Hell, I could do that job, and I would get things done.* This was a direction he had not previously considered, but the idea started to make him think that maybe he could make a difference. With continued encouragement from his pal, Zack, his family, and his friends, he'd decided to run to fill the vacancy in the Senate left by Harding's death. To his surprise and delight, he'd won.

He'd run as a Republican, just to the right of center, and received nearly sixty percent of the female vote. That helped him get elected and it didn't hurt that he was tall, dark, and handsome.

Analyzing his win, Will had thought about his upbringing. His mom and dad had been supportive of everything he wanted to do. It was just that he didn't know what he'd wanted to do. With this win, he had begun a new direction in his life. *Maybe being a United States Senator was what he had been looking for. We'll see*, he'd thought.

Now that he was in the Senate, it was not at all what he expected. Will was always a get-things-done kind of guy. Unfortunately, that was not how Washington worked.

Will came out of the bathroom and sat down behind his desk. There was a stack of mail to read and phone calls to return, and, as he expected, Christie was still there waiting for him. She continued reviewing the agenda with the senator and gave him the highlights of the schedule for the next few days. Will stopped her and said, "I need some time to gather my thoughts before the vote. Please give me five, will you?" Christie left the office and quietly closed the door behind her.

CHAPTER 7

CHRISTIE ADAMS

Will returned to his office after the vote. It was about six thirty in the evening. Christie was still there and waiting for him to sign some important papers.

Christie Adams was a smart, pretty brunette standing five feet seven inches with shoulder-length brown hair and beautiful blue eyes. She'd been a runner-up in the Miss Maryland beauty pageant. Christie's family, her father a doctor and her mother a teacher, lived in the Baltimore area. She was an only child and had graduated from George Washington University with a degree in political science.

Her first job had been for a lobbyist on K Street. She'd hated it! She'd kept her eyes and ears open, and when a position became available in Congressman Charles Ryberg's office, she'd applied for it and gotten the job. She'd worked with him until he'd retired seven years later, enjoying the excitement of working in the political arena.

Two years ago when Will Thomason, the handsome new senator from Florida first came to DC, he was a hot topic of discussion for most of the female staffers. When a friend told her that he had been looking for an aide, she'd interviewed for the job and was hired. Most of the female aides in the Senate were very envious of her.

Christie, at twenty-nine, was six years younger than the Senator. When she met him, she'd thought she was in love; now she knew it! He was a good-looking and smart guy with a great personality. They had a good relationship that got better with each passing day. Christie was his right arm and always watched his back. No one got past this gatekeeper!

After Will signed the papers she'd placed out in front of him, he put down his pen and looked straight into her eyes. .His mind was thinking how hot she was.

She smiled at him, noticing his face was, for some reason, turning slightly red. She sexily twirled a piece of her hair around her index finger.

"Are we done for today?" he asked.

"It depends. Done with what?" she said as she crossed her legs and looked back into his eyes.

"With work," he said a little intimated by her boldness. "I'm starving."

With a twinkle in her eye, she coyly asked, "for what?"

A little flustered, he answered, "Food. Come on, let's grab a bite."

Christie answered "okay" as she stood and headed for the door.

CHAPTER 8

THE THREE

Charlie's Bistro was the favorite restaurant for many of the area's crowd. It was just a short walk from Will and Christie's office building. Many aides and staffers met there after work to socialize, have a few drinks, and gossip about the latest scandal.

The dimly lit restaurant was warm and welcoming. The bar, which ran down the entire left side of the room, was filled with the friendly chatter and laughter from an animated group of regulars. The room itself had an elegant, slightly sexy aura. Burgundy upholstered booths lined the back wall. Smaller tables and chairs filling the rest of the room. The walls were covered with signed photographs of famous senators and congressmen and a few celebrities, too. Soft music played in the background. Christie and Will looked around for a place to sit. The restaurant was packed.

"Hey, Senator, over here." Will turned to see his old friend, Zack Miller sitting in a nearby booth. "Join me! Plenty of room."

In a place like this, a senator always attracted attention. However, if you were Senator Will Thomason, you were treated like a rock star. Everyone seemed to think there was something special about this guy; they wanted to say hello to him. He shook a lot of hands and kept smiling. Flashes were going off from cameras as he waved.

"Can I have your autograph?" Zack asked teasingly.

I guess these people have nothing better to do, Will thought as he and Christie sat down to join Zack.

Will and Zack went back a long way. They'd met in college at the University of Florida. Both were avid Gators fans. They'd attended all the home games together and even travelled to some away ones. Football was king in Gainesville. After graduation, Zack had gone on to law school, and Will had gone into the marines. They'd remained good friends. Distance could not diminish that.

Zack was a little shorter than Will, at about five foot ten, with light reddish-brown hair and a twinkle in his clear blue eyes. His family owned a paper mill in North Florida. He'd grown up in a beautiful, old house in a prestigious area of Pensacola. They appeared to be quite comfortable, and although it was never mentioned, Will always assumed Zack was a trust-fund baby.

By the time Will's election was over, Zack Miller had already been living and working in DC for almost five years. He was a top attorney at Grey, Doolittle, and Marsh. It was one of the largest law firms on the east coast. He earned a six-figure income, lived in a beautiful apartment near DuPont Circle, and was a very eligible bachelor. Zack knew that being single right now was a good thing. He would have a hard time splitting his time between work and a wife.

Christie was greeted by Zack with his usual, "I hope you've decided you are now ready to marry me." She laughed at the old joke and, as usual, said she would have to give it some more thought. And again, they all laughed. As she excused herself for the ladies' room and left the table, both men's eyes followed her, watching her sexy walk.

Zack said, "Are you two hooking up yet?"

"She works for me, Zack. I can't fool around in the office. I must admit, though, sometimes she makes it very difficult for me to ignore her flirtations."

"Then fire her…and *marry* her! You are not going to do any better than Christie Adams."

With a little more seriousness in his voice, Zack said, "It's good to see you, buddy. What's been going on?"

"Just a long and frustrating day," Will replied.

"It looks like there's something more than the usual on your mind. Do you want to talk about it?" Zack asked.

"This Surveillance Camera Bill is driving me nuts. It's a bad bill for all of us, but I don't see how I can stop it. Senator Holloway is just too powerful. He has strong connections in both houses. This is a bad bill. It's just a bunch of crap and I feel so frustrated.

Zack did not say a word.

Christie returned to the table and moved in next to Will. The conversation between the two friends ended. They ordered dinner and drinks and enjoyed the rest of the evening. Zack kicked Will under the table several times and teased him about Christie. She was used to these two. There was always a lot of ribbing and laughing whenever they were all together.

CHAPTER 9

DEAD IN THE WATER

Will Thomason arrived at his office at about seven thirty in the morning to get some work done before the staff came in.

About an hour later, Christie walked in. "Good morning, Will. What are you working on?" she asked. Without waiting for an answer, she continued. "We have two bills to go over, and you have an appointment at ten thirty with Congressman Wilson from Georgia." The phone rang. The staff began arriving and entering his office to talk to him. And so another day began.

Whenever Rhett "Bubba" Wilson (R-Georgia) entered an office, everyone in the building knew it. He garnered a lot of attention wherever he went. He was a large man, at six feet six inches tall and 290 pounds, with a booming voice. He'd played linebacker for the Georgia Bulldogs and had spent eight years as a professional football player with the New York Giants before he broke his leg and was forced into retirement. Bubba Wilson was asked to run for office because of his name recognition. The party was right: he won in a landslide. The congressman was now in his second term and very popular.

Whenever he entered the office, the women all turned to the congressman with smiles on their faces and waited their turn for his bear hug. They all liked Congressman Wilson. He was a fun and good guy, a true standout in Congress.

"Where is that young marine?" Will heard the booming voice ask as Bubba entered the office.

He rose to meet Bubba. "How have you been?" asked Will as the two shook hands.

"Fine, my man," he replied in his southern drawl as he sat down across the desk from Will.

"Would you like some coffee?"

"Okay, that sounds good."

Before Will could buzz for Christie, she entered with a small tray and two coffees, both black, no sugar.

"Good morning, Congressman Wilson, how are you this morning?" Christie asked as she handed them both their cups of coffee.

"I'm great," he responded.

After Christie left the office, Bubba said, "That's some aide you got there."

"Yes, she is. I don't know what I would do without her," he said, ignoring the innuendo.

"Will, I guess you heard about Senator Webster."

"Yes, I did. What a surprise. Just like that, he's gone. It makes you think."

"You know, his bill will be dead in the water now," stated Bubba.

Will agreed. "Thank God. It looks like we put this one off, but what a way to do it. May he rest in peace," Will said.

Bubba began, "I have two bills I want to get through Congress. I will need your help in the Senate."

"Okay, let's talk about them." They worked well together and after a lengthy discussion, Will promised his support, and the congressman left.

CHAPTER 10

A DAY OFF

*O*n *crisp fall days, playing golf is a priority. Work will wait*! That was the philosophy of Senator Vern Holloway (D-Maine). Whether he was at home in Maine or in DC, golf had always been a priority

Holloway had graduated from Harvard University and Harvard Law School. For the past twenty-five years, he'd represented the state of Maine in the Senate. He'd served on many committees during his long tenure and six years ago was elected chairman of the Homeland Security and Government Affairs Committee.

Sitting in his sunroom overlooking the magnificent grounds of his five-acre Virginia estate, the senator was drinking his morning coffee and thinking about the great weather. *There are not any votes today—perfect for golf.* After making several calls, he arranged a foursome for eleven o'clock. He informed his office and his aide, Julie Madison, "If you need me, you know where to find me." He knew that since most of the staff had worked with him for years, they would not be surprised by his call.

The Oakridge Golf Club, with only 150 members, was the oldest and most prestigious country club in the state of Virginia. The thirty-six-hole golf course was beautifully manicured and meticulously maintained. The old clubhouse had warm wood paneled walls, a cozy bar and comfortable seating. He had enjoyed many great meals with the other members at this five-star restaurant.

As he arrived in his black Cadillac Escalade, he was greeted by the parking attendant. "Good morning, Senator." Holloway had been a member of the club for over twenty years. Everyone knew what he expected and catered to him—*and* he was a good tipper.

He headed to the locker room to meet with his golf buddies. This was not just a locker room. It was an amazing maze of rich maple lockers with brass name plates and imported Italian-marble floors. In the center was a large spa, surrounded by showers. Massage tables occupied the corners of the room.

He had played golf with the same group of men for ten years, a bunch of doctors, lawyers, businessmen and congressmen. They had a lot in common. They were all affluent and successful at what they did and liked to take a little time off to play golf.

The foursome changed and headed out to where their golf carts and clubs awaited them. As he climbed into his cart, the senator thought, *Golf, a good cigar, and a couple of beers... life is great!*

The senator's car was parked at the far end of the private parking lot, away from prying eyes.

As the cool wind whistled through the trees and the leaves began to fall, a car pulled up next to the Escalade. The side van door slid open, and someone got out and crawled under the front of the Cadillac. The figure was slight enough to fit under the transmission section and reach the front wheels. The person opened a small bottle and squeezed its contents over a section next to the right wheel. After waiting a while to make sure the bottle's contents were doing their job, the person closed the bottle, wrapped it in a towel, and put it back into the bag. The figure slid out from under the car and drove away, thinking, *this is a beautiful golf club. I may learn to play golf just to be in a club like this one.*

CHAPTER 11

THE MEETING

A beautiful sixty-five-story office building in Midtown Manhattan sat on Fifth
Avenue near Fifty-Ninth Street. The outside
was dark glass and reflected all the buildings
near it. The sight from the street was amazing
and the view of the city even better. On the
top floor were a set of offices paneled in dark
walnut with marble floors. Gold trim adorned
throughout. The gold plate to the right of
the solid walnut double entry doors read, "S.
C. INC." This penthouse floor could only
be reached by the elevator with a special key
card. Most people thought the building had
only sixty-four floors.

Tonight there was a lot of activity on that
top floor. The conference room, surrounded

by windows, offered a spectacular view of the city. Seven men were sitting at a large, round conference table for their quarterly meeting. There was a lazy Susan with all kinds of wonderful food, and the bar on the side wall was fully stocked. The members were enjoying the food and drinks while chatting in small groups at this quarterly meeting.

William Goshman, the chairman of Electromagnetic Corporation. With 450,000 employees, the corporation is the largest manufacturer of electronic components in the world. Their main office is in Boston, Massachusetts.

Jonas Bottoms lll, the CEO of Pacar Mechanical, Inc. It is the country's largest manufacturer of earth-moving equipment, with headquarters in Gary, Indiana.

Duke Marcus, the chairman of Cason Oil Company, the largest oil company in the world, with 525,000 employees, is headquartered in Dallas, Texas.

J. Donald Vista Jr., chairman of Vistamark Stores, Inc. They own the largest number of retail stores in the world and support over 1.2 million employees. Their headquarters are located in Batesville, Mississippi.

Karl Strass, chairman of Glenworth Financial Corp. With $1 trillion in assets, they are one of the largest investment banks in the world. Their headquarters are located in New York City.

Trent Loggings, chairman of Gillian Software. Their software can be found in almost every computer in the world. They are headquartered in San Francisco, California.

Frederick Grey, senior partner at the law firm of Grey, Doolittle, and Marsh. They are one of the largest law firms on the east coast. Their main office is in Washington, DC.

Mr. Grey is this year's chairman of the Solution Committee. This position rotated annually between its members. At exactly seven o'clock, Frederick Grey tapped his glass with a knife to get everyone's attention. The room became quiet immediately. "Before we start our committee meeting, we have an important subject to discuss this evening," he said. "Last week I got a ticket from a traffic camera on Fifth Avenue…"

CHAPTER 12

THE AUTOPSY

John Reed had been with the FBI for almost twenty years. He'd applied right out of Hofstra College on Long Island in New York. He'd then attended the FBI training facility in Quantico, Virginia, and graduated top in his class. His first assignment had been in the Cleveland, Ohio, office, where he'd spent five years chasing white-collar criminals. He'd had a great conviction rate. From there he was sent to the Washington Field Office (WFO) in DC, and he had been there since.

Reed stopped by the medical examiner's office to get the results on Senator Webster's autopsy. While waiting for Dr. Jonas Hill, the chief medical examiner, he looked around at the office's plain light-green walls, metal desks, and linoleum floors. *At least we have carpeting in our office*, he thought. For many reasons, this was not the warmest place to visit.

Dr. Hill entered. He had been in DC for twenty-eight years, and had seen it all Reed knew. "Hello, Agent Reed, how are you these days? How are the kids doing?"

"They're fine! Josh is in the eleventh grade now and wants to go to Georgetown. He'd better get a scholarship!"

"I know exactly what you're saying, John. Wow, the kids grow fast, don't they?" the doctor said.

"Yep, time flies," he replied.

"So what can I do for you today?" Dr. Hill asked.

"I would like to see the autopsy report on Senator Samuel Webster," Agent Reed requested. "I know it was a heart attack. I would just like to double-check. You know me, Doc."

"Okay, let's take a look," Dr. Hill said as he pulled the file and started reading through it.

He looked up at Agent Reed. "It appears that he died from a heart attack but we did find a very small puncture in the top of his right shoulder. It could be nothing."

Reed wanted to know, "Is it like a needle hole?"

"Maybe," Doc said. "I have to look at the body again to be sure before it goes to the funeral home. I have a few minutes, so I can do it now."

"Mind if I come along?"

"Not at all. Come on." They walked down to the autopsy room, and Dr. Hill opened the drawer that held the body of Senator Webster.

Dr. Hill pointed to the small hole under the magnifying glass.

"It's amazing that you found such a small puncture," the agent said as he watched the doctor. "If that's a needle hole, what was in the needle?"

The doctor replied, "It's more of a pin prick, but I will run some tests to check for any drugs that might have been in his system."

"Maybe he did die from something other than a heart attack," Reed said. "Let me know, Doc."

"I will, Agent, as soon as I get the results."

Special Agent John Reed was a good investigator. He took nothing at face value. Senator Webster had been in good health for his age. He'd had no history of heart trouble or any other major medical problems. *It just seemed odd*, John thought as he headed back to his office.

His cell phone rang. It was his wife, Beth. "Don't forget, you need to be home by six tonight," she said. "Maryanne and Mike are coming for dinner, and I need your help."

"Okay, honey," he replied as he hung up the phone.

John and Beth had been married for almost eighteen years and had two children. Josh was a junior and Heather was a freshman in high school. They both were "A" students and on the honor role. They had their mother's blond hair and good looks. Beth had done a good job of raising the kids.

He and Beth had met in Cleveland. She'd been working for a law firm that was defending an accountant who stole a million dollars from his clients. John couldn't take his eyes off the pretty, petite blonde. Finally, after months of working on this case with her, John had mustered up the courage to ask if she would give him her phone number. She said yes, and they'd dated for almost a year before he asked her to marry him. She said yes to that too.

CHAPTER 13

THE FED

Will Thomason entered his office after winning an early-morning vote on a highway-transportation bill. Pleased, he thought, *we just need the president to sign it now.*

His secretary, Margaret, handed him a bunch of messages. He read them as he walked into his office, and before he could even sit down, Christie was there. She had a habit of sneaking up on him. "We have a lot to do, Senator."

He thought, *when have I heard that before?* Then said "It's good to see you too."

"You have lunch with two reporters from the *Washington Post*. You promised them an interview today about why you are fighting the Surveillance Camera Bill."

"Oh, yeah, okay."

The phone rang. Christie grabbed it and then handed the telephone to Will. "It's Special Agent John Reed from the FBI."

"Hello John, who are you investigating now? Not me, I hope."

"Well, all you senators are a little shady, but no." He laughed. "Something important has come up, and I was hoping to discuss it with you today, maybe at lunch?"

"Hang on a minute." He covered the mouthpiece with his hand. "Christie, will you change my appointment with the reporters and set it for later this week?"

"Will do," Christie said, "But it's important that you meet with them, you know."

"Yes, I know, but something more important has come up, and another day would be better." Will removed his hand from phone and said. "Okay, John, come on over to my office around noon. We will go to the Senate dining room for lunch."

"Wow, I feel important! I'll be there."

Almost two years ago, when Will Thomason had just been in the Senate a short time, he'd met FBI Special Agent John Reed and they'd become friends. At that time the agent had been investigating the death of Senator Joseph Harding (D-Florida), Will's predecessor.

Will had told him, "The reports said that the senator died from a heart attack."

John had been a little suspicious of Harding's death but nothing could be proven.

Harding had supported President Hutton who had been trying to close Gitmo (Guantanamo Bay in Cuba) ever since he was elected. Congress had taken away the funding to close the jail and the President could not proceed without it. Harding had been working hard to get the funding put back into the budget.

The Florida senator had also been supporting bill S-2143 at the time of his death. The bill proposed to reinstate the funding—$150 million—to move the prisoners from Gitmo to an empty state prison in Utah. The bill died with the senator, and Gitmo is still open.

CHAPTER 14

LUNCH

At about noon, Will and Agent Reed entered the Senate dining room. It had a nice atmosphere with its white tablecloths and carpeted floors, and was a great place to see many of the DC elite. "Wow! This is your lunch room." said the agent. "We have vending machines in ours."

As they sat at a small table in a private corner and looked over the lunch menu, John asked, "Do you remember our discussion a couple of years ago on the death of Senator Harding?"

"Yes, I do. Why?"

"Well, I've been looking at a few things, and I think a pattern may be forming," John said.

At that moment, the waiter came by and took their order. After the interruption, John Reed continued, "Harding was trying to get that Gitmo funding bill passed. You were against that, right?"

"Yes, I was, but remember: I wasn't a senator at the time."

"Okay, right," continued the agent. "And when Webster was trying to pass a health-care bill for illegal immigrants, you were his number-one opponent to that bill, weren't you?"

"Yes," Will replied. "Where are you going with this? Do you think I had something to do with their deaths?"

"No," John said, "but it is a bit of a coincidence. You've been against their bills. They died; their bills died. See what I mean?"

Will was a little irritated. "As I said, I wasn't a senator when Harding died. A lot of senators were against those bills. Aren't you taking a big leap?"

"No I'm not, Senator," John responded. "I think I am onto something. I'm not sure, but

I just can't let it sit without a little further investigation. You know, the FBI doesn't believe in coincidences."

Lunch arrived---a couple of sandwiches and the famous senate bean soup. They began eating and chatted for a few minutes before Will asked, "Do you have any proof?"

"No, just a gut feeling. Something isn't right." Looking at Will with a half-smile on his face, John continued, "You know, that is one way to stop the bills you don't like."

Will was not smiling as he said, "That's insane. Think about what you're saying. I wouldn't say a word of this to anyone. They will think you have lost your mind and will put you in the nuthouse." Will thought back to Congressman Bubba Wilson's remarks from a couple of weeks ago regarding the same thing, and thought, *two people I know and respect have similar thoughts on the subject. That's a little disturbing.*

"I am not *that* crazy, Senator. I'm waiting for the autopsy results from the medical examiner."

Will said emphatically, "John, it was a heart attack—nothing more!"

"We'll see," the agent replied.

Lunch was over, and both men had a long day ahead of them. As they rose to leave, Agent Reed said, "We'll talk soon. Thanks for lunch." Then he added with a smile, "Are you fighting any other bills that I should know about?"

CHAPTER 15

THE JOB

Frederick Grey was having a very busy day. He had a court appointment and meetings with two clients. Grey is the chairman and senior partner at the law firm of Grey, Doolittle, and Marsh. There had been times lately when he considered retiring. *From college to here, where had the time gone? After forty years of practicing law*, he reasoned, *I should be thinking about retirement, but I still love being an attorney.*

After his meeting with a new client had ended, he was ready for a drink. He turned to the bar in his office and poured a glass of Chivas Regal scotch, his favorite, and took a sip. *Ah! This hits the spot.* He picked up the phone and asked Zack Miller to come to his office. He turned his chair to the wall of windows overlooking the Capitol. *I will never get tired of this view.*

Zack entered the office and asked, "You wanted to see me, boss?"

"Some view, isn't it?"

"Yes sir, it is. Quite beautiful."

"Have a seat," Frederick said, turning his chair back to his desk. "Want a drink?"

"No thanks. I'd never be able to get back to work."

"What have you heard from Suzy?"

"She's working hard and doing a great job for us. She told me she wants to learn how to play golf."

"I bet she would be good at it," Frederick said.

"That she would! She's good at everything she does," replied Zack.

Frederick continued, "It may be time to speak to your friend. What do you think?"

Zack said, "It may be. He is getting frustrated with the way things work. He's a tough guy and works hard to get results. I'll feel him out over the next few days. I have to go carefully. While we're on the subject, sir, maybe we should slow down a little. This next incident will be pretty close to the last one. We don't want to arouse any unnecessary suspicions."

Grey hesitated a moment. "I will discuss your concerns with the committee and we will make that decision. You just do your job and let me know how you make out with your friend."

"Yes sir," said Zack as he stood and left the office.

CHAPTER 16

GOLF, A DANGEROUS GAME

Senator Holloway's estate and the Oak Ridge Golf Club were about eight miles apart. It really was an easy drive. The senator had made that trip one thousand times in the twenty years he had been a member.

The valet brought his car up front and opened the trunk for the golf clubs. He opened the car door for the senator. For that he got a ten-dollar tip. Vern Holloway thought, *that's a lot of money. After all, he's just a valet.*

He'd had a good day playing golf with the guys, having lunch and maybe a few too many beers. He knew he was fine to drive home on this tree-lined, winding road overlooking the valley below. With the beautiful view of the countryside, he looked forward to this part of his trip home every time he left the club. He knew the curves in the road like the back of his hand. He could have driven them blindfolded if he had to.

He was about halfway home when he approached a big curve in the road. He touched the brake a little too late to slow down and pulled the wheel hard to the left to stay on the road. He hit the guardrail, and the car slowed a little. Panic set in as he realized the car did not turn along with the steering wheel. As he saw that beautiful view of the valley get larger, he thought what a great picture it would be hanging over his fireplace. The car hit some small branches of the trees lining the road. Then everything was upside down, and his seat belt was tight around his chest. He saw the trees and the sky. It felt like he was floating in midair. There was a loud crashing sound. Then black.

CHAPTER 17

THE COMMITTEE

After Zack Miller had left his office, Frederick Grey sat back and thought about the committee and why it had been formed. It had been right after the last election. He thought back to when Senator Colby Marcus had approached him one afternoon at his office. Colby had been having a bad day and needed to vent. He and Frederick had been friends for more than twenty-five years.

"What's going on, Colby?" Frederick had asked.

"I'm just having a bad day. There are times when I get so frustrated that I can't stand it. Since we lost the election and control of the Senate, President Hutton has pushed this country so far to the left. There are more regulations than anyone can handle. The EPA is going wild, and this

so-called health-care law…Anyway, I'm sorry for ranting, but I just had to talk to someone. During the past few weeks, I have been thinking about a solution to these problems. I want your opinion, just between us."

"Okay," replied Frederick. "Let's hear it."

"I was thinking…What if we form a committee of the smartest and the richest businesspeople in the country. They will need strong balance sheets to help finance our program. We want people who are as concerned as we are about our country and its future. There shouldn't be any more than seven members. They will vote in our committee to choose which up-and-coming bills may adversely affect the direction of the country. And then we can focus our influence in Congress to derail those bills."

"So, the committee votes? Then what? You do realize a vote is no good without consequences."

"Yes, I know, Frederick. That's the key to this committee. We will do anything to get the congressional votes changed—anything!"

"Just exactly what does anything mean?"

"Just what it sounds like," Colby replied. "Anything! We have to change the direction of this country any way we can. Listen, Frederick…if this fails, the whole world loses! There are four years until the next election. This president could destroy the country in that time. Drastic times call for drastic measures."

"Wow," responded Frederick. "What happened to the Constitution?"

Colby had answered, "The Constitution was formed through revolution. Remember?"

Looking at his old friend, Frederick was stunned. "I am going to need time to think this over, Colby," he replied. "You're really blowing my mind. Just for the sake of asking, who do you want on this committee?"

"First I want you, said Colby. I'm sure we will need a good attorney. Then we can research the largest companies in the United States and see who thinks the way we do and would have the most to lose if things kept going in the direction they are now. Small businesses are being hurt by new regulations. It affects jobs. Large corporations, like multi-nationals, have the highest taxes in the world. Actually, they are double taxed. That's why they leave their foreign profits overseas. This has *to change, we need money here! We will quietly approach their CEOs separately and feel them out. We need seven for a majority vote. Think about this, Frederick. You know everyone. Come up with a list of the top businesspeople with a big stake in this country and who want to make a difference."*

The phone rang and brought Frederick back to the present. His secretary reminded him of his next appointment. As he headed out of the office, Frederick thought about his talk with Zack Miller and made a mental note to discuss Zack's concerns with the committee. He would also add to the agenda a discussion about Zack's friend and his potential for the committee.

Back at his office after his meeting, Frederick Grey's thoughts again focused on the Solution Committee. *Looking back over the past year, he was pleased with his accomplishments as the head of the committee. Yet there was so much more to do to stay on top of the situations. Turning U.S. into a socialistic country, like Europe, would destroy most jobs. The free social programs would bankrupt us. Look at Europe today, two percent growth is considered great. In order for America to prosper, we need four percent growth year after year. That's how to build great wealth. Then we can help everyone. This country is too important to the whole world to fail. He just couldn't let that happen!*

CHAPTER 18

THE RESULTS

D r. Jonas Hill had just received Senator Webster's blood report back from the lab. After removing the liver and the stomach, he read the tox screen and saw the blood was clear as well. *Hmm*, he thought, *along with the clean report on the hair and urine, this is just a heart attack. Or perhaps whatever was used to kill the senator has already dissipated.* He sat back and gave some thought to what type of poison could kill quickly, not show up in the toxicology report, and disappear from the system within days. He did a little research, and then he saw it: strychnine poison, absorbed after administration into the skin, could take up to an hour before having any effect. After thirty-six hours, levels were too low to be detected. The senator had died forty-eight hours ago.

Agent Reed was back at his office that afternoon when Dr. Hill called. His secretary took the call and passed it to him.

"Hello, Doc. What's up?"

"I just received the report back from the lab. It was clean: no poisons or drugs."

"I need something, Doc—*anything*," said Reed.

"Well, I did a little research. If someone put strychnine into whatever made the pin hole, it could have killed him and not left a trace after thirty-six hours. But I have no proof, and I found no trace of anything in his system. Sorry, Agent. No help, I'm afraid."

"Okay, Doc. I'm disappointed, but thank you."

On his way home, after a very busy day, Reed thought, *Nothing! Bubkes! Shit! I thought I had something.*

He arrived home in time to help Beth set the table for dinner with their friends. She looked good, and he really needed to get his mind on something other than work. He gave her a big kiss, and she looked up at him. "What's that for?" she asked.

"You just make my life better," Reed said. "What kind of wine do you want?"

CHAPTER 19

THE ACCIDENT

It was Friday morning and Agent Reed was in his office early. It had been a busy few weeks and he was enjoying the quiet before the beginning of another day. As usual lately, his thoughts drifted back to the senators' deaths. *I still haven't received anything to corroborate my suspicions. Unfortunately, the only real way to get results is to do additional testing on future victims. Wow, how macabre! I am becoming crazy over this. I have to let it go. Will is right...I better not mention this to anyone.*

And then, later that afternoon, John received a call from Captain Pete Jones with the Virginia State Police."

Reed picked up. "Yes, Captain, what can I do for you?"

"I'm at an accident scene on Country Road Fifty-One, about three miles from the Oak Ridge Golf Club."

"Captain, you know the FBI doesn't get involved in auto accidents."

"Well, you might want to look into this one. The victim is Senator Vern Holloway."

John just sat there, stunned. Maybe he'd misunderstood. "What did you say?"

"Senator Vern Holloway is dead. His car went off the road at the sharp turn overlooking the valley. The car is about two hundred feet down the incline, and the body is badly burned. I will let you know what we turn up."

"I'm on the way," John said. "I'll be there in an hour."

As he headed to his car, his mind was swirling. *How could this be a coincidence? Who the hell is killing off these senators? All three deaths have been different.*

What do they have in common? he thought as he drove through DC into Virginia. *Let's see: all powerful senators with long tenure. They were all Democrats with bills in work. Shit, that's it! Will thought I was crazy, but I bet he won't think so now. I need to find out what the bills were about.*

He noticed the flashing lights up ahead and slowed down to find a place to park. There were skid marks on the ground coming from the direction of Oak Ridge Golf Club. *That means he hit his brakes.*

Captain Jones approached Agent Reed. "That was quick."

"Thanks for calling me, Pete. What do we have here?"

"Well, you see the skid marks. Follow them into the trees and down the incline for about two hundred feet. The car exploded at the bottom. It's a real mess. My guess is that he was going a little fast around the turn and skidded off the road and went over the guardrail."

John went over to the guardrail, bent down and looked at the damage caused by the car hitting it. He saw the bend in the rail from the impact. He then stood and looked over to where the car landed. He was checking to see if they all lined up. They did.

"The Senator had just left the club. Maybe he'd had a couple of drinks—who knows? We will talk to his golf buddies, and I will know more when we get the body to the morgue and the car to the impound garage."

"Do me a favor, Pete. Have the medical examiner do a toxicology screening for strychnine."

"You think he was poisoned?"

"I don't know. Just checking."

"Okay, will do," Captain Jones replied.

"Call me when the car is back at the garage. I would like to take a look at it."

Reed surveyed the area once more before getting into his car and heading back to DC.

On the way to his office, he called Senator Will Thomason. The secretary informed Reed that the senator was in a meeting, and she promised to tell him about Agent Reed's call when he returned to his office.

CHAPTER 20

HIS AIDE

Senator Will Thomason was heading back to his office after a transportation committee meeting when he was approached by Democrat senator Carter Devine.

"Hey, Will, I understand we are on the farm bill budget committee. Let's get together for lunch next week."

"That sounds good, Carter. I think I'm free on Tuesday, but I will have my secretary confirm with yours."

"Good, see you then," Carter said as he headed for his office.

Will thought, *that budget for the farm bill is going to be a bear to trim. Maybe Carter will help...fat chance!*

Now, back in his office, the pace was slower than usual. No one was attacking him when he got there. Christie was at lunch, so he had a little time to think about the transportation meeting he'd just left.

Will started to think about Christie and back to what Zack had said, "*Fire her...and marry her!*" He had no intention of firing her, but marrying her? *Maybe*, he thought, *they could get just "a little closer"*. He was really turned on by her and he thought she knew it. He was conflicted. *I don't really have time for romance, but if not now, when? I don't know what to do, but I guess it's stupid to ignore it, he* reasoned.

A few minutes later, Christie entered Will's office. "I'm back from lunch. Did you miss me? How did your meeting go?" she asked.

"Good and yes, I did miss you," Will answered again torn by his emotions. "See, I have nothing to do?"

"Well, then, I'll just have to fix that," Christie replied.

"Really," Will said. "What do you have in mind?"

"I don't want to embarrass you," she said, smiling at him as she headed for her desk to gather the information she needed to discuss with him.

He thought. *She does this to me all the time!*

CHAPTER 21

CONNECTING THE DOTS

The intercom buzzed. "Senator," Margaret announced, "Agent Reed is on line two."

"Hey, John. What's up?" Will asked as he answered the phone..

"Senator Holloway is dead!"

"What?" Will said with astonishment. "When did it happen?"

"He was on his way back from playing golf this afternoon. His car went off the road in Virginia."

"Oh, that's terrible," Will said.

Reed asked, "Do you remember what we were talking about at lunch a few weeks ago?"

"Come on, John, you don't really think there is a connection with Webster's and

Harding's deaths do you? Both senators died from heart attacks, two years apart, and this is a car crash. I think you're getting paranoid."

The agent answered, "Dr. Hill told me that Senator Webster's death could have been by poison."

"Well, did they find any signs of it in their systems?" Will asked.

"No, nothing."

Will continued, "Then what are we talking about here? Two senators dying within six weeks of each other doesn't constitute a conspiracy."

Reed replied, "It's bothering me. I am going to investigate a little further, just to be sure."

"It sounds crazy to me, John, but if it makes you feel better, let me know how you make out."

John Reed just knew something was going on. He could feel it. *I just have to put it all together*, he thought. *I know I will find something.*

CHAPTER 22

MINORITY LEADER

Christie stepped into Will's office. "Minority Leader Marcus just called."

"And?" Will asked.

"He wants to see you in his office."

"Okay, when?"

"Now," she answered. "What do you think is going on?"

"I don't know, Christie."

"Senator Marcus is the minority leader. He wouldn't call you into his office without having a good reason. Something's going on."

"Then I guess I should go and find out."

"Okay, Senator, I will be waiting here for you."

"See you in a bit," he replied as he headed for Senator Marcus's office.

As Will entered the minority leader's offices for the first time, he observed their elaborate setup. They were twice or maybe three times the size of his and beautifully furnished.

The senator's aide, Liz, interrupted his thoughts. "Hi, Senator. How are you? Senator Marcus is in his office. Please go right in," she said as she showed him the way.

Following Liz, he could not help himself from observing the rich, dark wood-paneled walls with elegantly framed pictures. Most of the photos featured the smiling senator shaking hands with important politicians and presidents from both parties. This gallery took prominence on the wall behind the senator's large, *U*-shaped desk. Above the soft brown-leather sofas were more personal photos of his family's oil fields in Texas. After shaking hands with Will, he offered him a seat in the brown-leather armchair across from his desk.

Senator Marcus spoke first. "I am sorry I haven't had the time to talk with you since you came on board. I try to touch base with all the new senators. Tell me, Will, how is everything going?"

"Good, sir," Will said. "I'm starting to get the feel of how all this works."

"Well, from what I hear, you're a fast learner. There is a lot to understand. This administration has really screwed up the economy and foreign affairs. We're in a real mess. Taxes are way too high and we can hardly keep up with all the new regulations."

"You are one of the most popular senators of the whole group, on both sides of the aisle." Marcus continued. "I have been hearing good things. I purposely delayed this meeting to give you the time you needed to get involved. I'm impressed, Will."

"Thank you, sir. I'm trying."

"You're a sharp guy, well spoken with a mind of your own. I have been doing this for a long time, son, as you know. I have seen many new senators and congressmen come and go. Most of them start out like a house on fire, and then they fade. Your enthusiasm has continued to grow."

Will replied, "I am proud of this country and everything it stands for. I am here to represent those people who elected me and to do it to the best of my ability. I learned that in the marines, and it is something I will take forward for the rest of my life."

"You know, Will, I was a marine too. Vietnam!"

"I didn't know that, sir," said Will.

"That was a lousy war, but then, all wars are lousy."

"Yes sir, I agree."

"In a year and a half, we will be electing a new president. I am looking for someone to support for the job. It should be someone who is young, smart, and dynamic. That person should have a real love for his country."

"I know you have a good background, even though you didn't graduate from Harvard," he said with a smile. "I would like to get to know you better. If you would be interested, we can get together from time to time to discuss our country's future."

"Yes sir, I would like that."

Minority Leader Marcus listened intently to what Will had to say. "You appear to be well versed on a lot of subjects." They talked for a few more minutes touching a little on foreign affairs and the economy.

"I'm glad we had this meeting." Senator Marcus stood, shook hands with Will, and escorted him to the office door.

Will left, happy to have been noticed by the senator but not quite sure what just happened. *Why did Senator Marcus ask me to come to his office? Why would he want the advice of a two-year senator? Seems a little strange*, he thought.

Senator Marcus dialed a number on his private cell phone. Duke Marcus answered, "Hello, Uncle Colby. How did your meeting go?"

Senator Marcus always enjoyed speaking with his nephew. He made business sound like pleasant small talk and he was a smart guy. He'd been running Cason Oil for eight years, ever since Senator Marcus' father and the last of his uncles, the original owners, had passed away.

"Fine. I liked what I saw."

CHAPTER 23

CONFUSED

Will made his way back to his small office. *That's why they all stay*, he thought to himself. *The longer you're here, the better office you get.*

Christie was waiting for him when he entered. "So what did he say? What did he want from you?"

"I don't know. I *think* he asked for my advice on the state of the country. He did most of the talking. I'm a little confused."

"Was anyone else there?" she asked.

"Just me. And he wants to have regular meetings to discuss what is happening and the future of the country."

"What did you say to him?"

I said, "Okay, we'll be talking." Then the meeting was over.

"Boy," said Christie, "he wanted to know what you think. That's great. But do you think anything else is going on? He's a politician, Will. I think he's got something up his sleeve."

"I have a feeling you might be right about the senator having an agenda. But what do you think it could it be?" Will asked. "Why do you think he's interested in me and my opinion? I've always wanted to make a difference, but not even in my wildest dreams could I have imagined that politics was in my future or that I would ever run for the Senate. But then again, I never thought about running for anything. I thought I would stay in the marines for life, not help to make policy for the whole country."

"You are quite a guy, Senator," Christie said. "You care about people, and you fight for your beliefs. That's what I like about you."

"I am kind of charming, aren't I?" he said smiling back at her.

"You're more than charming," Christie said.

Will answered, "You're not so bad your-self," as he stood and began moving towards her.

"Not so bad!" Christie replied as she stood, putting her hands on her hips.

He replaced her hands with his as he drew her close and kissed her lips.

"Wow! That was unexpected, but nice."

"Then let's lock the door and continue."

"No. There are too many people around," said Christie.

Will leaned in and passionately kissed her again.

Christie felt a chill run through her body but stopped him. "Not here," she said.

"Okay, Will said grudgingly. I already have plans to meet Zack at Charlie's for dinner. Join us and we can go back to your place afterward and continue this discussion."

"That sounds good, but let's go now," Christie replied. "before this goes too far and besides, I'm hungry."

CHAPTER 24

THE APPROACH

Frederick Grey was in his office when his private line rang. "Do you have a moment to talk?" Duke Marcus asked.

"Yes, let me close the door. Okay, I'm back. What's up?" Frederick asked.

"My uncle had a talk with your guy today. He told me it went very well."

Frederick interjected, "So it appears we are going forward with *his support?*"

"Well," said Duke, "Uncle Colby would like to have another meeting with him in about a month. At that time, we can make *the* decision. We may have to postpone Zack's approach to this issue with his friend."

"I understand what you're saying; I'll take care of it," Frederick replied and hung up.

Frederick asked his secretary to call for Zack Miller, and Zack arrived a few minutes later.

"Good morning, Zack. Take a seat. I just want to see how everything is going."

"Good, sir."

"Have you spoken with your friend yet?"

"No," Zack said. "I was planning to call him today."

"We may have to hold off on that for a little while," Frederick said.

"Why?" Zack asked.

"Senator Marcus had a talk with your buddy yesterday. They chatted about our country's future and plan to meet again in a couple of weeks. Anyway, let's not bring anything up right now. Show him your support, Zack, but let him tell you about his meeting with Senator Marcus. We want to get his impression of the meeting before we speak with him."

"Okay, whatever you say, sir. I agree with a more cautious approach right now," Zack replied.

CHAPTER 25

THE FINDINGS

The next day, Dr. Jonas Hill reviewed the autopsy report on Senator Vern Holloway. He noted that a toxicology assessment was also performed on the senator. Just then, Captain Pete Jones came into his office. "Good morning, Doc."

"Good morning, Captain. Is there something I can do for you?"

"I am here for the autopsy report on Senator Holloway," Captain Jones replied.

"I was just reading it," the doctor explained. "Why did you order a toxicology assessment?"

"Agent Reed requested it. The Feds are being thorough, and he asked me to follow through."

"Oh. Okay, I was just wondering. He died from a broken neck, burns and smoke inhalation caused by the crash and explosion. The tox screen was negative."

"So I guess we have an accident, then," Captain Jones said.

"It looks that way, Pete."

"Okay, thanks, Doc. I'm out of here. I'll let Agent Reed know the findings."

From there, Captain Jones went to the state garage holding area where the car had been towed.

What a mess, he thought when he first saw the wrecked vehicle. *No one could have lived through that.* "Mike, the investigating mechanic at the garage was halfway across the floor, wiping grease from his large callused palms. Hey, Mike, what did you find on the senator's car? Anything I need to know?"

"Well, it looks like he broke the front right tie rod when he hit the curb too hard on that turn," replied the mechanic. "He would not have been able to turn the car back onto the road. It appears the senator hit his brakes too late to stop the forward motion. He hit the curb, broke the tie rod, and went over the side."

"Did you make sure there is nothing else that could have caused the crash?" the captain continued. "What about the break in the tie rod? Are you sure it was from hitting the curb, not being cut?"

"No way to tell after the fire," Mike answered. "What are you asking me? Do you think this wasn't an accident?"

The captain answered, "I'm not saying that. I just want to be sure."

"Well," Mike replied. "The tie rod broke from hitting the curb. There was no bushing in the joint connection. If it was gone before the accident, it could have broken more easily, but there is no way I can know that. It also could have burned up in the explosion."

"Was there a bushing on the other side?" Pete asked.

"I couldn't find it in the rubble," Mike said. "There is no way to prove whether the bushing was there or not when the wheel hit the curb."

"Okay, thanks, Mike." As the captain walked back to his car, he questioned why Agent Reed was so suspicious of this accident. As he got into the car, Pete dialed Reed and gave him the results.

John threw his pencil across the room. "Are you sure? I'm so frustrated I can'tbelieve that this was just an accident. I know there has to be something!"

CHAPTER 26

FRIENDS

Christie and Will entered the restaurant for dinner with Zack. It appeared he was not there yet. They found a booth in a private corner. Christie slid in and Will followed her on the same side of the booth. They chatted for a few minutes, careful not to show any display of affection. Gossip in this town ran wild. The tiniest hint of any news went viral in seconds.

Zack arrived and sat down across the table from them. The three laughed and talked awhile about the usual Washington chatter. After ordering dinner, Christie excused herself for the ladies' room and as usual they watched her walk away.

When they were alone, Zack said, "There's something different about you tonight. What's going on?"

"Well, Christie and I did have a little talk and kind of agreed to work on our relationship."

"That's great. I knew you two would get together sooner or later. I hope you didn't postpone anything tonight because of me."

"No, not really," Will said. He leaned closer to Zack. "There's something I want to discuss with you. Senator Marcus called me into his office today. Can you believe the senator wants to discuss the future of the country with *me*? What do you think he really wants?"

Zack, expecting Will to tell him about the meeting, showed no surprise at the news. He replied with, "I always knew you would be a standout here and some of the important people would take notice. That's why I encouraged you to run for office. You're an asset to the party, and I think the senator sees that."

Christie returned to the table and they ordered dinner. They continued discussing the DC politics and again dabbled in the latest gossip. All the while Christie and Will shared secret glances knowing tonight was not going to be like any other night they'd ever had. When the bill finally arrived, they said their good-nights and left. Outside they hailed a cab and cuddled in the back seat, kissing and groping each other like teenagers.

Within a few minutes, they arrived at Christie's apartment. As they entered, she turned and grabbed Will and kissed him with wild abandonment. Clothes started flying. They worked their way into her bedroom, half naked. The passion that had been building for the last few months, released itself. They made wild love a few more times before falling asleep.

Christie was lying on her side with her eyes on her new lover. She was feeling happier and more contented than she ever had.

CHAPTER 28

THE PARK

Zack Miller's dog, Stokes, was a strong, sixty-pound, three-year-old black lab. When he saw his master get the leash, he got all excited. Only Zack could control him when he got like this. It was time for his after-dinner walk to the park. It was dusk and a cool night for a walk. Zack grabbed a jacket.

When they arrived at the park, there were a few other dogs running and playing in the field. Zack threw a ball and released Stokes, who took off like a bullet, running after it. He found a bench and sat down to watch Stokes and the other dogs.

Zack heard footsteps. Someone was walking on the path behind him. She stopped at the bench and sat down next to him. He didn't look up.

"Your dog really loves it here, doesn't he?" asked the woman.

"Yeah, this is his best spot," Zack answered. "How did you like the golf club?"

"It was a beautiful place—tight security."

"Did you have any problems?" he queried.

"No," she replied.

After another few minutes, he called, "come on, boy, let's go." He put the leash on Stokes, and they headed home without a goodbye to the woman on the bench. He knew she'd sit a few minutes longer, eliminating any suspicion that they were anything but strangers in the park.

CHAPTER 29

SUZY AND BEN

The Mediterranean Sea was a clear, deep blue. The sand was almost white. The beauty abounded in not just the sand and sea. Suzy was stunning in her tiny white bikini. Even though there were a lot of beautiful women in Tel Aviv, Suzy stood out. She sat down and lay back on a chaise lounge to get a little sun. After lying there for a few minutes, Suzy felt a shadow fall across her face. "You're late," she said and looked up at the figure standing over her.

"I have been here for ten minutes watching you put on that show you do when you're waiting for me. I must admit—I love it." Ben Lehman had been in love with Suzy since they'd attended Harvard together. They'd met in their freshman year and had been a couple ever since, though sometimes from a distance.

Suzy, an adorable baby, had been born to a Chinese father and French mother. She'd been educated at the finest private schools France had to offer. When she was very young, she learned martial arts from her father and found she was very good at self-defense. It had come naturally to her. At sixteen she earned her black belt. At seventeen, she had been accepted into Harvard. Suzy Lu had always been an over achiever.

After they'd graduated from Harvard, Ben had gone back to Israel and joined the Israeli Mossad, and Suzy had gone on to Harvard Business School. After earning her MBA, she'd traveled to Israel to join Ben. She wasn't ready to start her career yet. She wanted to spend as much time with Ben as possible, but with his job it wasn't easy. She had been in Israel for three months. Now it was time for her to start thinking about her career. She realized it could take her away from Ben again.

Suzy had an insatiable quest for knowledge and wanted to know everything about what Ben was doing. He had tried to explain that what he did was top secret and there were things he could not tell her. That only piqued her curiosity more.

She met Ben at his office one afternoon for lunch. When she arrived, he had been in with the boss, Sidney Bloomberg, and she had to wait in the outer office. After the meeting Ben and Sidney, walked out to meet her. Ben kissed her on the cheek and made the introductions. With that, he said, "I'll be right back. I have a quick errand to run."

Sidney invited Suzy to his office to wait for Ben. They talked about a lot of things, finally getting to Suzy's future. She told him she had been taking a little break to decide on a direction for her career. He knew, from what Ben had told him, that she was smart. She had loved intrigue and was looking for something exciting to do. He listened to what she was saying, and thought *she and Ben were made for each other.* He asked if she had given any thought to becoming an investigator. That type of job would tick off many of the boxes of what you are looking for. He had a friend in DC who was managing partner for a large law firm. Sidney liked this young woman and would be happy to make a call to his friend to see if he could use someone with Suzy's qualifications.

Suzy was thrilled with Sidney's offer and could not wait to tell Ben.

When he returned a few minutes later, she relayed the conversation, thanked Sidney for all his help and they left for lunch.

CHAPTER 30

THE LOVERS

Ben and Suzy had worked on different continents for several years. They maintained a long-distance relationship and were still madly in love. Ben leaned down and kissed her—a long and passionate kiss. "Let's get into the water," he said. He took her hand as they headed toward the sea to cool off from the summer heat. After a half hour of swimming and playing around in the water, they headed to her hotel room. They had been apart for a couple of months and were making up for lost time.

A few hours later, while they were dressing for dinner, Ben asked, "Tell me, what you are doing for this committee you work for?"

Suzy walked up to him, turned her back. "Zip me up, will you?"

"Let's skip dinner," he said as he kissed her neck.

"Later Ben," she said. "I'm starving."

"Okay. I am too, but I know what I want for dessert." She giggled and they left the room.

The restaurant sat right up on a high cliff. It wasn't large, maybe twenty small candlelit tables with white tablecloths. There was a cool breeze, and a full moon lit up the night. Their table was near the edge overlooking the water. It was the perfect, private setting they loved.

"I want to hear all about your job," Ben said.

"I want to hear all about your job as well," said Suzy.

"You know I can't talk about what I do, Suzy."

"Yeah, I know, but neither can I."

"I saw in the paper that Senator Vern Holloway died in a car crash," said Ben. "He was a pretty important senator, wasn't he?"

"Yes, he was."

"How did you do it?" Ben asked.

"Do what?" Suzy asked.

"It's me you're talking to. I know your work," he said.

"Are you asking me for details?" she asked coyly.

"Yes. Maybe I can use it in the future," he replied with a smile. "We will talk about it later," she said, as they ordered dinner. They ate, drank, talked, and laughed the night away. Then they headed back to the hotel room to continue what they'd started earlier.

As they lay in bed, she said to Ben, "We must talk about some things I'll need before I return to the states. It may be good for both of us."

Before he could reply, she started kissing his ear and worked her way down, She was all over him in seconds.

CHAPTER 31

OVAL OFFICE

President William Hutton, a Democrat from Kentucky, and his political adviser, Matt Fulton, were sitting in the oval office at a meeting prior to his reelection committee's arrival in the conference room.

"So what's going on inside the beltway?" the president asked.

"Well, sir, you know that Senator Holloway died yesterday?"

"Yes, I heard. That's a big loss for us. What happened to his surveillance camera bill?"

"For right now, it's dead in the water," Matt replied. "But we are trying to resurrect it as we speak."

"Who do we have for Holloway's replacement?"

"I am waiting to see how the governor handles it. As a Republican, if he opts to make the appointment, we could lose the seat."

"Stay on top of this, Matt, and keep me informed."

"Yes sir."

"What else?" the president asked.

"I heard a rumor that the Republican leadership is seeking a young up-and-comer to run against you in the election. Right now it's just a rumor, but I'll keep an eye on that too."

"Who do you think it could be?" the president asked.

"Don't really know yet, sir. I'll let you know as soon as I hear something."

"Okay. You know we only have eighteen months until the election. They are going to need a real dynamo if they want to win in this short period of time."

"I think we're in good shape, Mr. President."

"We're only in good shape after we win! Don't forget it."

"Yes sir."

The president's secretary entered the office. "Mr. President, the committee is ready for you."

Following the meeting, President Hutton came back to the oval office. He had a meeting with General Stone Black, head of the joint chiefs.

"What's going on, General?"

"Well sir, the new president of Iran is pushing hard to complete their nuclear program. It looks like a year, at best. We have to do something, sir. Also, there is Syria. President Remard is crazy. This war will not end till we end it!"

"That's not going to happen, General. Let them kill each other."

"Sir, the Israelis will not stay passive much longer."

"Sure they will. They need us to move forward. They won't make a move without our help."

"I'm not so sure, sir. We just can't keep sitting back and watching."

"Why not?" the president asked.

"Sir, if this war spreads to the Suez Canal, the price of oil will double here at home. It could affect our economy."

"No, it won't. We will build more solar and wind power and use less oil and coal. The people will accept higher prices for cleaner air and not having to go to war. That's our policy, General. Any questions?"

"No sir."

CHAPTER 32

THE STRATEGY

Suzy turned over to Ben lying next to her. She leaned in to kiss him. His eyes opened, and he smiled. "I could do this forever," he said and climbed on top of her. She looked into his eyes, and the fun started all over again.

An hour later, as Suzy got out of the shower, she called to Ben. He was on the phone, just hanging up as she walked into the bedroom.

"Who was that?"

"We have to talk," he said.

"You look so serious," she replied.

"I am."

"Okay. I knew this was too good to last," she replied.

"Our military is putting together a plan to go into Iran and Syria. They are not waiting for the United States any longer."

"What are they going to do?" Suzy asked.

"I don't know yet, but it will be big," Ben replied.

Suzy was quiet for a while. "Why does it have to be big?"

"The world has to know we will not be killed again like with the Nazis."

"You know, you can do it quietly and say you know nothing about it. Everyone will know it was you, but they will have no proof," Suzy said.

Ben looked at her. "What are you talking about?"

"I thought you were smarter than that, Ben. I guess I am going to have to teach you a few things."

"Like what?" he asked.

"Like keeping thousands of people from dying by just killing one person and not having a war."

"What do you have in mind?" Ben asked.

"Well…what if we could put a plan together to secretly take out both presidents quietly, at night, when no one is looking?"

CHAPTER 33

THE DECISION

Jonas Bottoms sat at the conference table, looking out onto Fifth Avenue. *No matter how many times I see this view, I am still awed by it. What a beautiful place Manhattan is.* Jonas, the chairman of Pacar Mechanical Inc., which was located in Gary, Indiana. He always looked forward to this quarterly trip to New York for the Solution Committee meeting.

"The big city always brings smiles to the faces of you small-town boys," said Karl Strass with a laugh. Karl, the chairman of Genworth Financial Corporation of New York. They all laughed with him.

Duke Marcus, of Cason Oil in Dallas, remarked, "Everyone knows that New York is a tiny place compared to Texas."

The ribbing was common at these meetings. They were always comparing who was from a bigger city, had more assets or employees, and so on.

"Okay, guys, it's time to settle down and get to business," said Frederick Grey, this year's chairman of the Solution Committee. "There are folders in front of you containing the biography of a possible candidate for president. I'd like Duke to bring all of you up to date on his recent conversation with his uncle, Senator Colby Marcus."

"It was a quick telephone conversation," Duke said. "It appears the senator has the person in mind for the next run for president in eighteen months. He is a young senator from Florida. His name is Will Thomason."

"He's a little young, don't you think?" said William Goshman, CEO of Electromagnetic Corporation. He looked over the biography in the folder and continued. "His lack of experience could hurt us in the end."

"I don't think so," said Grey.

Trent Loggins asked, "Is he smart enough to learn the ropes in just eighteen months? Do you think he will work with us to win the White House?"

"Yes, he is very smart," answered Grey. "He spent thirteen years in the marines and knows the constitution by heart. He is very popular and will be great on the campaign trail. We have a close connection to him through one of my attorneys, Zack Miller. They went to college together and have remained very close friends. It was Zack who convinced Thomason to run for the Senate. On top of all this, Zack will help us keep an eye on the senator."

"Are there any other comments?" No hands went up. "Okay, then let's think about it over the next couple of days and do our homework. We will need to hold a special meeting next week. Be prepared to discuss this further. We need a decision by the first of next month."

"Good. Now, moving on, we have other business to discuss. I heard from Suzy. She is in Israel…"

CHAPTER 34

THE INVESTIGATION

John Reed sat at his desk at the Washington Field Office. He reviewed all the information he had compiled and realized he had nothing! Bubkes! Junk! He couldn't go to the Department of Justice with this. He thought, *I have to call Senator Thomason. Maybe I should speak with both Senator Holloway's and Webster's staffs first. That's the place to start.*

After meeting with Julie Madison, Holloway's aide, and discussing the senator's surveillance camera bill, he came away with nothing he didn't already know.

FBI Special Agent John Reed finally reached Jennifer Riley, Senator Webster's aide, and headed over to meet with her.

"Why is the FBI investigating the death of Senator Webster?" Mrs. Riley asked Agent Reed as they sat down in Senator Webster's office.

"It's just standard procedure," he replied. "Can you tell me which bills the senator had been working on most recently?"

"Well, the main bill was Health Care for Immigrants S-2673. It was a very partisan bill. Republicans wouldn't go near it, and the senator had been fighting with his own party as well."

"So there was no chance for this bill to pass?" Agent Reed asked.

"No, actually there was. You had to know the senator. He had a lot of contacts, and he kept a book detailing events over the past thirty years. He had names, dates, and, well, photos of people in bad situations."

"Where is the book, Jennifer?" Agent Reed asked.

"I don't know. He was very secretive about it and never showed it to me. I just heard him talking about it."

"Are you saying Webster had enough information on others to get this vote passed?"

"Yes, I guess I am, Agent Reed. Do you think someone killed him because of this?"

"I don't know. I'm just looking for information right now. What else can you tell me?"

"Well, two things: First, Congresswoman Marline Dewhurst is sponsoring the bill in the House this time. I'm not sure where she's at with it. Second, I hear that the senator's replacement will probably be a Republican appointed by Governor Arnold."

Something else to consider, John thought. "Do you think Dewhurst has the senator's diary?"

"I don't know," Jennifer replied.

"Thank you for your time and the information," John Reed said as he stood to leave.

As he was walking out of the senator's office, Reed asked himself, *What have I learned from Jennifer? Not a lot of answers but a lot more questions. There are more suspects, for one thing. Does Congresswoman Dewhurst have the book? Could Webster have been killed because they wanted to replace him? I really must be going crazy.*

The next stop was Congresswoman Dewhurst's office. She'd been a good friend of Webster's and might be able to shed some light on the information Agent Reed had just learned.

"She's out of town. She'll be back next week," said her aide.

Of course I can't speak with her. Why would I expect to get some real answers? This town could drive anyone to the bar for a drink. Charlie's, here I come.

CHAPTER 35

THE THEORY

Zack Miller was eating dinner at Charlie's when John Reed entered. He spotted Zack sitting in the corner and went over to say hello. Zack invited John to join him, which he did. The two had met last year at a Christmas party given by Senator Thomason. "So what's happening at the FBI?" Zack asked.

"Funny you should ask. I am working on the senator's death."

"Which senator?" Zack asked.

"Well, both," answered John.

"Both?"

"Senators Holloway and Webster."

"Since when does the FBI investigate heart attacks and accidents?" Zack asked.

"We don't. It's just a theory I'm working on."

"What's your theory?" Zack asked as he motioned to the waiter. Agent Reed ordered a sandwich and a beer. "Boy, you Feds eat well." Zack laughed.

"Remember: I'm a government worker on a fixed salary, not a high-priced attorney."

"So tell me your theory."

"Well, I just want to be sure of the findings, that's all. You know how the FBI is."

"And how many other deaths are you investigating?" Zack asked with a hint of sarcasm.

"I'm looking into Senator Harding's death too."

"Harding?" Zack asked. "That was years ago."

"Three to be exact,"

Zack looked up and stared at John Reed for a minute.

"How did you come up with that? You really had to reach for that one. Is this what the American people pay you for? They could cut your pay, or, worse, fire your ass. But don't worry. I'm your friend and won't tell anyone."

"I'm serious, Zack. This is not a joke."

"You're nuts, John! I'm an attorney. Tell me all the facts you have to prove this *theory* of yours."

"I have no proof, just coincidences. But in my business there are *no* coincidences. Someone or some group is killing these people. Take a look at the senators who died. Look at how their deaths have changed the direction of the laws being passed. This is real, Zack."

"Directions are always changing when bills are passed. That's how our system works," said Zack. "Three deaths don't make a conspiracy, especially over a three-year period. You should back up and take another look at each death. Remember: one was an accident and the other two were heart attacks. It just sounds a little far-fetched to me. I wouldn't talk to anybody about this." John got his sandwich and started to eat. Zack finished his dinner and had another drink. "I know it sounds crazy," John said, "but something is wrong with these deaths. I just know it."

"Okay," Zack said. "Putting on my lawyer hat, let's look at each senator. First, Senator Harding. He was seventy-one years old, had had heart trouble in the past, and drank like a fish. If that lifestyle didn't kill him, there would be questions. Now, let's look at Webster: seventy years old, enjoyed living high in Congress for thirty years. Younger men than him have died from heart attacks. And Holloway spent twenty-five years in the Senate, eating and drinking his way to the top. What was his alcohol level when he died? He had just left his country club, John, after playing eighteen holes of golf and, I'm sure, drinking all the way. No connection, as far as I can see. I think I'm a pretty smart attorney, but without anything more than a hunch, I can't see the validity of your suspicions. And, like I said, it's just too farfetched."

"Yeah, yeah, yeah. I know you're probably right. Maybe I am thinking too much into this," said the Agent.

"Maybe," Zack replied with a laugh. They had a few more drinks and a few laughs before saying their goodnights and heading home.

When Frederick Grey entered his office the next morning, Zack Miller was waiting for him. "Good morning, Zack. What's brings you here this morning?"

"Last night I had dinner with Special Agent John Reed of the FBI. He has a theory," said Zack, and he proceeded to relate to his boss the conversation from the previous evening.

"So you don't see anything to substantiate his suspicions and have made sure he understands that, right?"

"I hope so," Zack agreed.

"Let's keep an eye on him, Zack. Hopefully you convinced him he was on the wrong track."

CHAPTER 36

THE BOOK

Marline Dewhurst (D-Oregon) had the H.R. 4302 bill in committee and was fighting to get Sam's through. It was an uphill battle. With Senator Webster dead and the elections coming up, no one could be persuaded to go forward. Marline was frustrated.

After returning to her office from a meeting, she was sitting at her desk, thinking about her next move, when the phone rang. It was Elizabeth Webster. "Why don't you come over tonight? We can have a relaxing dinner and catch up a little."

"Sounds good to me," said Marline.

Marline arrived at six o'clock. It was nice to get together with her old friend. Elizabeth made a great pot roast and salad. They talked about the old days and had some good laughs. After dinner they went out to the patio for coffee and dessert. They enjoyed a little "girl talk". Marline expressed her frustration about getting Sam's bill through committee. "I don't have the same relationships that Sam had with these people, and I don't know how to get them to move. How did he do it? Did Sam have any files or anything here at home that might help?"

"You know, Marline, he had a bunch of boxes in the back office. I haven't done anything with them. I'm having a hard time going through his things, and I haven't wanted to go into his office alone. Would you mind doing this with me?"

"I know, Elizabeth, I can only imagine how difficult it must be for you. I miss him too. Okay, let's do this together. Come on."

They went into the old office and started opening a bunch of boxes in the corner. About halfway through the mess, Marline found a book, stopped, and opened it. "Elizabeth, look at this. This book has names and addresses of senators, congressmen, and lobbyists, with notations. It dates back twenty-five years." Marline knew most of the names. "Look at this: 'Senator Carter Divine has a bastard child. She would be about nineteen years old now. I bet his wife doesn't know!'" Information like this filled the pages of the book.

Marline thought *Sam was a son of a bitch. That was how he got all his bills passed and was so successful in the Senate.* She said, turning to Elizabeth, "we are going to use this to get Sam's last bill passed and then forward it to President Hutton before the election. What do you think?"

Elizabeth said, "You know how important this bill was to Sam. If you think it will help you get it passed, do it."

Within a couple of weeks, the votes seemed to be going Marline's way. It looked like the bill may make it out of committee by next week.

Zack had been following this bill. It was just about dead two weeks ago; now it looked like it may get out of committee. How? Something had happened. He started making inquiries around the House, but no one wanted to discuss it. So he pushed harder, and one night, on his way out, he cornered Mike Douglas (R-Texas) in the elevator. "Mike, tell me what's going on with Dewhurst's H.R. 4302 bill."

"What do you mean, Zack?"

"Come on, Mike, we've been friends for a long time. How could this get out of committee so fast, if at all?"

"Let's talk over here, Zack," Mike said as they exited the elevator and headed toward a quiet corner. "The word I hear is that Dewhurst has something on a couple of congressmen and said she would use it unless this bill was passed. Don't know who or what, but the buzz is that its information Sam Webster had that Dewhurst has now. You know that she and Sam's wife, Elizabeth, have been friends for years. Maybe that's where she got it. A lot of people are not happy, to say the least."

"What do you think it is? Do you think it could be some kind of a list or diary?" asked Zack.

"I think it's a book or some kind of a list with information that some very important people do not want to have revealed. I'm sure some of those people would pay a lot of money for that book."

Zack's mind was racing, and he knew what he had to do.

CHAPTER 37

I GOT IT

Suzy had just landed at Reagan International Airport. She was walking through the terminal when she received a text. "Will be walking Stokes at 7 tonight. Join me."

Stokes was having a good time running around and catching his ball when Suzy showed up.

"We are looking for a book," Zack told her. "We think it contains damaging information about several important DC politicians. We don't know where it is, but we think Congresswoman Dewhurst has it. Once we find it, we can stop the vote."

"Get me her information, and I'll check it out," Suzy said.

Marline Dewhurst was getting nervous. A lot
of people were pissed at her. *How did Sam get
away with this?* She thought. One congressman
had threatened her, and another had told her
to watch her back. She'd promised to throw
the book away after the vote was complete, although she knew she wouldn't. She was enjoying the power.

After several days of searching, Suzy told
Zack that she had not found anything. She'd
searched everywhere except Congresswoman
Dewhurst's office, which she could not get into.

Zack thought about it. "Maybe it's still
where Sam kept it hidden. Could it still be at
his house? She may have reasoned that if it
was a good place for Sam to keep it all this
time and no one had discovered it, then that's
where she would keep it."

Suzy agreed to search the Webster home.

At seven o'clock the next night, Suzy
watched Elizabeth Webster leave her house.

Ten minutes later Suzy entered Elizabeth's
house and looked around. It was a big house,

and she checked each room carefully. She was heading into the old back office when she heard a noise. She quickly ducked into a small closet and waited to see who was there. As she peeked through the crack in the door, she realized Elizabeth Webster was home. Suzy looked at her watch. It was only eight thirty. *Who goes to dinner for less than two hours?*

Suzy watched as Elizabeth headed toward her bedroom. A few minutes later she came back into the living room wearing her robe and slippers. It was apparent that she had gotten comfortable for the night.

Shit, Suzy thought. *Now what do I do?* Right at that moment, Elizabeth's phone rang. "Hello, Marline, how are you? Yes, it's in the same place we left it. Why? Okay, I'll check." Marline headed for the back office. From her view in the closet, Suzy watched as Elizabeth retrieved the book from its hiding place in one of the boxes.

"It's right where I said it was," Elizabeth said into the phone. "It's safe. Okay, I'll put it back. Don't worry, Marline; no one will find it." She hung up, put the book back, and left the room.

I*s this luck or what?* Suzy thought. She quietly left the closet and tiptoed across the room to the box that held the book. She took the book and checked it out to be sure it was the one. Without a sound, she opened the window and slipped out. *Whew, a close one*, she thought as she got into her car, which was parked at the end of the block.

Zack was watching football, relaxing, when he received a text. "Got it," it said. *This is going to be a good game*, he thought.

Two days later, Zack was in Frederick Grey's office reading over the book that Suzy had retrieved from the Webster home.

"Wow!" Zack said. "This is almost too hot to handle."

"The point here is to stop Dewhurst," said Grey. "And a lot of this could help us in the future."

"Yes sir. I'll go to work on it."

CHAPTER 38

WORLD ORDER ISN'T EASY

"I want to go over Suzy's report. We have a decision to make," said Frederick Grey. As he read the report to his committee members, he looked for their reaction to it, seeing a few questioning faces. After he finished explaining the plan to assassinate two world leaders, he opened the floor for comments.

"This is going to take some thought," said J. D. Vista, chairman of Vistamark Stores. "This may not be the time for us to tackle something this huge."

"We know it has to be done," said Trent Logins of Gillian Software. "If not now, when?"

"I suggest we just concentrate on the election for now and look at this again next year," said Duke Marcus. "This election is the most important project we have going on right now. It is a must-win for us. We don't need any distractions."

"I tend to agree," said Grey. "Who else has any input? Karl, what do you have to say?"

Karl Strass, Genworth Financial' s chairman,, said, "If we do this now, the financial markets will surely crash. Do we want that to happen just before the elections?"

"I think he's right," said J. D. "It could have an adverse effect on the election."

"Good point," said Trent Logins. "One thing we should all take into consideration is that Israel is involved with this, not just us. What will their reaction be?"

Everyone was quiet for a moment. Then Karl Strass said, "Let us take a vote."

"Okay," said Frederick Grey. "All in favor of proceeding with Suzy's plan raise your hand…" No hands went up. "All in favor of tabling this vote until next year…" Every hand went up. "Okay. The motion passes to hold this vote until next year."

"I'll have Zack Miller talk to Suzy about our decision. She will have to put her plan on hold for now and explain our decision to the Israelis. I'm sure that won't be an easy task, but I have confidence that she will be able to convince them that a delay is in the best interest of the whole world."

"Now, with that vote decided, let's proceed with our election plans and discuss each of our responsibilities for securing the nomination and election of our guy for president."

CHAPTER 39

ON HOLD

The next day Zack Miller was summoned to his boss's office.

"Good morning, Frederick."

"I want you to contact Suzy and inform her of our decision to put a hold on her plan until after the election."

"Okay, but it's not just Suzy's plan. Ben Lehman and the Mossad will not be happy."

"They will have to understand the situation. We're involved with the upcoming election," said Grey. "Suzy will have to persuade Ben that this is the right thing to do at this time. We don't want any operations in the Middle East until after the election."

Suzy called Ben to tell him of the decision from the committee to hold off till next year because of the election.

The message he received was not what he wanted to hear. Ben had to go back to his bosses and tell them the plan he'd put together was not going to work at this time. He understood the reasoning, but he looked like a jerk to his boss—at least he thought so.

"I know you're upset," said Suzy. And threw him a kiss over the phone.

He ignored her attempt to soothe him and said he had to go.

Remember she said, "You have to convince them of the value of this hold up. The plan would happen next year with the backing of the United States."

In the Middle East, confidence in the American government was dropping by the day. The Israeli's didn't believe a word President Hutton said anymore. He never backed up his commitments. The United States had a vital interest in stopping Iran and their allies because they represented a guarantee of weapons of mass destruction proliferation. This left the US allies in turmoil. As Iran took two steps toward nuclear capabilities, the Americans took two steps backward. This left the Israeli's to take matters into their own hands. Israel would have moved forward if not for the Solution Committee's request to wait. Ben Lehman had done a good job. It would always be in Israel's best interest to have the Americans with them. They decided to wait until after the American presidential election before taking any further steps. They hoped the committee's man would win, and maybe, through their US organizations, they would do a little more than hope.

CHAPTER 40

STRONG BACKING

Senator Colby Marcus, a Republican and the minority leader, gathered his leadership group together to discuss the upcoming election. "I want to know if anyone has a prospect for president." They were discussing the subject among themselves, but no one specific name was mentioned. Marcus raised his hand to call order in the meeting. "I have someone I like, and I'm thinking about backing him." There was total silence in the room.

"Who is it?" Senator Johnston asked.

"Senator Will Thomason," the leader responded. Again, the room was quiet, and then everyone started to talk at once. He had to call the room to order again. "One at a time, gentlemen."

"He's a little young, don't you think?" Senator Smithfield called out.

"Not a lot of experience—he's only been a senator for two years," Senator Bryant said.

"Pretty sharp guy though," said Senator Almeteri. "He was a captain in the marines. I hear he's a tough guy, takes no shit. And besides, the ladies love him and I think he could win that vote easily."

"Well, what do you think? It could work with the right backing. He's an all-American guy," said Marcus. "He knows how to speak from his heart about his country. As a marine, he has sworn to protect us. Think about him standing at a podium with American flags flying in the background, and him speaking about love of country. This would be hard to beat."

"Yes it would," said another senator. "But does he know how to handle the office? Does he have enough experience in running the country?"

"How about James Babcock?" said another senator? "He has a lot of experience and has earned his shot."

"Senators," Marcus said, "it may be Babcock's turn, but we haven't been too successful, in recent times, doing things the way we always did. The question is, who can beat President Hutton? I think Thomason can. We can help him with all the other things. Well, what do you think?"

Again, a lot of discussion and disagreement. Then the room went quiet as Marcus started speaking. "Let's talk about this and try to come to a consensus, gentlemen. We have to pick the right man for the job. We all know how important this decision is. So let's try to resolve this by our next meeting."

Two weeks later, at the next meeting, the senators had all done their research and answered many of the questions that had been bothering them. They continued discussing the issues, and after an hour, the decision was made by a substantial vote. Senator Will Thomason was their choice.

"Let's keep this to ourselves for now, at least until we speak with Senator Thomason and he accepts our endorsement. He can then inform the RNC of his intentions and make his public announcement," Senator Marcus said.

CHAPTER 41

THE PRESIDENCY

It was seven thirty in the morning, and Will was in his office early. He began reading his mail from the day before. He heard the door open, and in walked Christie. "What are you doing here so early?" asked Will.

"We have so much work to do. I needed an early start," she answered.

"I'm glad you're here. I have something to discuss with you."

"Oh, what?"

"Last night I met with Senator Marcus again. Remember the last time we met?"

"Yeah," said Christie.

"Well, you're not going to believe this, but the Senate leadership wants me to run for president."

"Of the United States?"

"You heard me," said Will.

"What did you say?"

"I didn't want to let him know how astonished I was, so as calmly as possible, I said I would think it over and get back to him."

"Are you sure you are ready for this?" Christie asked. "This is a huge step for you to take with such little political experience. You only have two years in the Senate."

"You're right: this is too crazy. They must be desperate."

"Are they?" she asked. "Maybe they're not. What is it they saw in you that led to this endorsement? Apparently they saw something! You are one of the smartest senators I know. You fight hard for what you believe in. Your constituency loves you, and I think you're pretty great."

"You do, huh? But is that enough for me to run for president? I always wanted to make a difference, but this?" Will asked.

"What do you have to lose?" asked Christie. *Wow, chief of staff to the president. Sounds good to me*, she thought.

"Let's get through the day and finish our work," said Will. "We have a lot to do. How about getting together tonight? We can discuss this further."

"Your place or mine?" she asked.

"Mine. You don't cook," said Will.

"Is that all you have on your mind: food?"

"Okay, your place," said Will. "I'll bring the wine."

The following morning, when Will entered his office, he asked Christie, "If I decide to do this, where do we start?"

"As of last night you hadn't made a decision," she replied.

"Well, last night I had other things on my mind," he said with a smile.

She just smiled back at him.

"When I finally got home and got to bed, I couldn't sleep. I tried to reason all the options, and if I pass on this opportunity, I may never get it again."

"Well, then, let's get started. First we'll need to find a good campaign manager and then a good speech writer," answered Christie.

"I can write my own speeches," Will said.

"No," she responded. "We need a pro."

"I *am* a pro."

"No, you are not," she said.

Will said, "Stop. I will write my first speech, and you will read it and tell me what you think. Okay?"

"Okay," Christie said. "But if it isn't good, I *will* tell you."

"I kind of figured that. We will have to keep as quiet as possible until we have our team in place. I'll talk to Zack and see who he knows on the street. He knows everyone. I guess the right campaign manager could be our biggest asset. Besides, Zack can keep me from making a fool of myself. I guess we've made the decision, huh?"

"I guess we have," said Christie. She walked up to Will and gave him a kiss. "We're in this together. Let's go."

CHAPTER 42

THE SPEECH

The next day Will had a little free time, so he decided to put together his thoughts and figure out how he was going to approach his candidacy. "Leave me alone for a while," he said to Margaret. "I have some work to do."

Now, where do I start? It took Will a couple of days to put together his thoughts for his speech, and it took another day for him to write it. *That was not bad*, he thought.

He began,

"My name is Will Thomason. I am a senator from Florida, and I am running for president. The world champion for freedom is the USA. We are a capitalist society, not a socialist society.

We believe hard work and opportunity for all will grow our country. I'm sure you've heard, a rising tide lifts all boats. You've heard that a lot. Seventy percent of all jobs come from small business. We must make it easier for these businesses to start and grow.

One of the most important areas to look at is energy. We should be drilling on all government land. Let's get these pipelines built. They are much safer than hauling oil by train. Just that alone will create thousands of jobs and freedom from foreign oil.

We must stop the all-political mindset we're in. Not everything *is* political. Maybe we should act strictly for the good of the people; we must go back to what the founding fathers wanted. It is your obligation to run for office, stay for a term or two, contribute, and then go back to your profession. This will let other Americans fulfill their obligations to their country instead of allowing a few to make government a career! Too many career politicians build empires and think they are above the law. *No one* is above the law. I will propose term limits for all congressmen, just like the limits for presidency. Two terms and you're out. I would like to see more young people with new ideas running for office. Here I am risking everything I have to help my country. Join me, let's do this together. Volunteer, vote out the bad politicians, help vote in the good ones, or maybe even run for office. Do something!

I propose a change in the federal income taxes. The system is a mess. I want to take a look at all foreign aid. We will help a country who needs it. Human rights and the rule of law are a must. I will not approve aid to a country to convince them to be our friend. They have to be our friend first.

I am a US marine and very proud of it. War is outdated. Nation building is outdated. But, I believe in a strong military.

There is no one who loves this country more than I do. I fought for it, got shot in the leg for it. I will protect us with my life if need be.

If you believe in what I'm saying, if you believe we need a change, if you love this country as much as I do, then give me your vote and your support. I need volunteers and your financial backing. For us to win, we all have to get involved. Tell a friend, tell a neighbor, or talk it up in the supermarket. Don't just stand there; do something! This is your country, so let's get to work!

Thank you for your support. God bless America."

I wonder what Christie will say?

CHAPTER 43

THE CAMPAIGN

As time went by, Will realized that running for the presidency wasn't the same as running for the Senate. Campaigning in all fifty states was exhausting. When he'd run for the Senate, he'd only had to make stops in Florida cities. Now he had stops in different states daily, sometimes visiting two or three in a day. This pace was frantic, and the press was constantly analyzing every word he said.

With about seven months of the campaign left to go, Christie was holding up well. As a matter of fact, she was the driving force of the campaign. They had assembled a good staff together, and the results were getting better each day.

The president was leading by seven percentage points. But the crowds were getting bigger and bigger at Will's rallies. When people met him, they loved him. The amazing thing was that he had not changed one bit since the beginning of the campaign. He told it like it was and made no excuses for any mistakes—and he made a few. He kissed babies, shook hands, and spoke with everyone at these rallies. The military loved him, and the women...they *really* loved him. He charmed them all.

He was surprised by the amount of money that was coming in. Big and small businesses alike were backing him to the hilt. What he needed now were the minorities. His speeches were getting better. His campaigning was getting better. He realized, *Maybe we have a chance—a small one, but a chance.*

CHAPTER 44

THE SOLUTION

At the next quarterly meeting of the Solution Committee, everyone was taking their seats. Frederick Grey said, "Let's get this meeting to order, gentlemen. The campaign seems to be going well. We need to talk about money. How much have we allocated for television, print, and radio ads? It's time to crank it up. We have a little over seven months left. Karl Strass has the numbers."

Strass stood. "Between us, we can put together about $1 billion for this campaign. I want to bury this president. It will take years to clean up his mess."

"I assume you have a plan to raise this money without the candidate knowing," Grey said. "Just because we've done well in the early voting doesn't mean this race is over."

"Yes," replied Strass. "I understand. All contributions will be going through a non-profit Political Action Committee, a PAC. It's already started. We're trying to buy all the TV time in as many states as we can. This will leave very little space for the Democrats."

"Good," said Grey. "That will drive them crazy. Do we have any other business?"

"Have any of you been listening to Congresswoman Dewhurst?" asked Bill Goshman of Electromagnetic Corp. "She just sponsored a new bill, H.R. 4302, in the House called Health Care for Immigrants. Does this sound familiar?"

"Yes it does," said Grey. "That was Senator Sam Webster's bill in the Senate. She is getting support to move it forward out of committee."

"What are her chances of getting it passed?" asked Goshman.

"Not very good. We just found Webster's book, and we are hoping that it will help kill the bill," said Grey. "Is there anything else?

No? Then I make a motion to close this meeting. Second? Yes, all in favor, meeting closed."

The following day, Frederick Grey passed the information on Congresswoman Dewhurst to Zack Miller with instructions to stay on top of the bill as it moved forward in the House.

Also, that afternoon, Grey spoke with Karl Strass, who informed him that Agent John Reed had been transferred to New York to investigate a financial scandal. The FBI had closed the investigations into Webster's and Holloway's deaths. They'd determined that Senator Webster had died of a heart attack and Holloway had hit the curb and gone over the edge.

"Good," said Grey. "That will keep him out of our hair."

CHAPTER 45

THE COMPETITION

Christie and Will had not had five minutes alone since the campaign had started. "I know it's hard, but we have to be very careful, more careful than usual. We cannot let anyone see us together until this is over," Will said.

"How about we go into the closet," Christie suggested.

"Ha! Ha! I love you, babe, but you know we can't do anything to upset the status quo. We have to get through this first and not give our opposition anything to attack us with."

The campaign pushed forward. Time was flying by, with only six months left, and the pace was frantic. Will was traveling from state to state, giving one speech after another. It appeared his message was getting through. The crowds were big, and his following was growing. TV ads and promotions were changing people's minds. The airwaves were flooded with his ads. You couldn't turn on your TV without seeing an ad for Will Thomason for president. If he won, it could be one of the biggest upsets in presidential elections, and some thought he just might.

President George Hutton was having a fit. "How can this guy be beating us? What the hell have you been doing?" he asked his staff.

"Sir," Matt replied, "the people love him, and it looks like he's spending five million dollars a day on advertising. He is everywhere. It's been difficult to buy air time in some states."

"Where is his money coming from?"

"All over. I think there are a lot of small donations, but it's mostly from big business. They are doubling what the unions are giving us. He is even getting the minority vote."

"How?" the president asked.

"He has convinced the people that our party has done nothing for them in the past fifty years and that he will change that. His push for new jobs in energy would affect all businesses. He's telling them that the help-wanted signs will be on every business from coast to coast. He is killing us," said Matt.

"I want you to check out his personal life, love life, and any other life he has," said the president. "He's single. Maybe he's gay; who knows? Find a boyfriend. Any dirt you can muster up or make up. I am not losing to some thirty-five-year-old jarhead."

Matt Fulton was beat up and pissed. "I will get a couple of investigators on this right away."

CHAPTER 46

THE LEAD NARROWS

The clock struck 10:00 p.m. as Will and Christie exited the elevator and headed to their rooms. They were both beat. He thought they were in Dallas but wasn't sure. The day had started at seven o'clock with a breakfast with a local religious group. Then there had been a luncheon, followed by a rally for about fifteen thousand friends and family. After that it was easy; they drove across town to a fundraiser and dinner with the rich and famous.

"What did we have for dinner?" Will asked.

"I think chicken," Christie said. "It was good."

"I didn't know. I never got to taste it."

"That's what the pain in my stomach is: hunger. I don't think I ate all day. How about we order up some room service?"

"Okay," Christie said. "I'll call from your room."

Will finally had something to eat and felt much better. Turning to Christie he asked, "What's for dessert?"

Christie responded by standing up and starting to undress. "Get those clothes off right now," she ordered. "Enough of this waiting."

They were naked in five seconds and at it like a couple of first-timers, climbing on top of each other. Will said, "You know, we need our sleep. Big day tomorrow."

"Screw sleep. Come here," she said. With a deep love and unbridled passion, they spent the night with their bodies intertwined.

"Well, now we know the senator is fooling around with his aide. These pictures should help. Too bad I couldn't get into the room." Bill Small was an ex–CIA agent who did snooping for a buck. And he was pretty good at his job. Republican or Democrat didn't bother him; it was all for the money.

Will and Christie woke up at seven o'clock to a knocking at the door. Christie grabbed her clothes and ran through the adjoining door to her room. Three people walked in, including Will's campaign manager.

Doug McGrath was a smart guy and had guided Will through all the ups and downs and strategies of campaigning. He'd taught Will how to act, how to dress, and how to articulate what he wanted to say without getting in trouble. He had an answer for almost everything Will asked him.

"Good morning, sir, we have some things to go over." *And another day begins*, Will thought. *When do these people sleep?*

"You look like you had a rough night. Are you okay?" one of his aides asked.

"Yeah, I'm fine. I ate late. It kept me up." He glanced quickly at the two plates. "Let's get started."

"Well, first, the latest polls show the president with a one to two percent lead. That's down from seven percent two weeks ago. We have them on the run, Senator."

"Wow, that's great! We might pull this off yet," Will said.

Zack Miller sat in his office, thinking about how to use the book without revealing that he had it. *Once Congresswoman Dewhurst finds out the book is gone, she will back off and the bill will die in committee...But what if she decides to go forward anyway? What they don't know will help her. So I have to convince her not to go forward. But how?*

President Hutton looked at the pictures of Christie Adams going into Senator Will Thomason's room. "So what?" Hutton said. "She's his aide, and her room is adjoining his. Is this all you have?"

"Yes," replied Fulton.

"Garbage," Hutton said. "Is this guy a boy scout?"

The private phone rang in Congresswoman Dewhurst's office. She picked it up. It was Elizabeth Webster. "Good morning, Elizabeth. What's up?"

"We have a problem, Marline. I can't find the book."

"What do you mean you can't find the book? I thought you had it locked up."

"I did," said Elizabeth. "It's not there. Then I thought I may have moved it after I spoke to you last week, so I started to look everywhere. No book. I don't know where it is."

"Could it have been stolen?"

"I don't see how. I have been here almost all the time. The only time I went out was when I met Ann for dinner last week, for two hours. That's it. I didn't see anything out of place. That was the night you called and I had the book. What are we going to do?"

"I don't know," said Marline. "I am getting a lot of pressure because of this book. I wonder if it's worth it. I'll give it some thought and let you know." She hung up and sat there, thinking, *What happened to that damn book? If it was stolen, who did it? Will they use it against me by telling everyone what I tried to do? This is a mess!*

It appeared the health-care bill would not leave committee as everyone had thought. "Congresswoman Dewhurst pulled the bill this morning, saying it needed more work," Grey said. "She will resubmit it again in the future."

"But I doubt it," said Zack Miller. He was settled in the comfortable chair in front of Grey's desk. "She's scared; she doesn't know how the book disappeared."

"Okay, good work, Zack. You got another obstacle out of the way. How's your friend doing?"

"As it turns out, he's a natural. The people love him. I'm having dinner with him tonight."

CHAPTER 47

TIME IS GETTING SHORT

"With the Senate race heating up in California, Carter Devine, Democrat, is doing better than expected," Frederick Grey said. "Is there anything we can do to stop him and help Harold Graham?"

"There might be. Graham has been in Congress for ten years and has a good chance of winning," said Zack. "But I'll look in the book. Who knows what we'll find."

"We need to win the Senate," Frederick said. "We need both houses to get things done."

"That could be a real challenge," Zack said. "But I'm on it."

The Democrats had a three-seat majority in the Senate. Twelve Democrats were up for reelection in November, along with five Republicans. The five Republicans seemed to be in pretty good shape to win. *Of the twelve Democrats running*, Zack thought, *we need at least four seats to go Republican so we can regain the majority. It would be nice to get more, but I can settle for the four seats.*

He thought the way to start would be to make a list of all Democrats who were running and the states they represented. Next, he'd see whether the states were red or blue in the last election. He'd research what the senators had voted for in the past six years, see if he could use the information against them. Then on to their personal lives: girlfriends, tax problems, and so on. *Once I find at least half of that group to be vulnerable, I'll check them out in the book*, he thought. *This is going to take some time, but it could be fun.*

Will Thomason was caught up in a whirlwind of fundraisers, luncheons, dinners, and large campaign rallies. All of this was mind-boggling to a small-town guy from Florida. There were four months left until the election.

The Fourth of July rally was going to be the biggest of them all. It was being held in DC at the National Mall on July 5, the day after the Fourth of July parade and fireworks display. The thought was to bring the people to the patriotic festivities so they would stay over for the rally. His marine buddies were coming with a few of their friends. He could not believe the amount of money he had taken in for his election. He hadn't realized that so many people wanted a change and wanted him to lead them. He felt this was a great honor, and he would not let them down.

Christie was his strength. Right after the election, win or lose, he was going to announce their intention to marry. One thing was sure: he was not going to lose her.

The polls were showing a tie at the moment. Now was the time to pounce hard! Will knew if they won the presidency along with the Senate, he could stop the fall of the country. He had put it all on the line, and he could not fail!

They flew back to DC for a small break before the fourth rally. They planned to meet Zack at their old stomping ground, Charlie's. "It's good to see you both again. It must have been three months since we last got together. How is everything going?" said Zack.

"It couldn't be better," said Will. "Christie and I are having fun. I will say that this is hard work and offers no privacy. As you can see, the secret service are all over. They lock us in at night and let us out in the morning. You didn't tell me about that part of it."

"It all comes with the job, Will. You'll get used to it."

"I am starting to put my policies together."

"Good," Zack said. "I want to go over them with you when you get a chance. Maybe I can contribute a little to your campaign."

"Okay, maybe next week after the DC rally. Do you know how the Senate races are going?" Will asked. "Do you think we can win the majority?"

"Yes, we will win, and so will you. You could be the best thing to happen to this country in a long time. Hey, am I getting a job in your administration?"

"I don't know," Will answered. "I have to do a background check first." It wasn't easy to say that with a straight face, so they all started to laugh.

"Yes, I want you as my personal attorney and adviser. It's probably a big cut in pay."

"That's all right. I'll suffer through it for you and country."

"What a great guy you are," said Will. Their dinner arrived and they laughed late into the night. Nothing had changed with these three, but could it continue?

CHAPTER 48

THE MOSSAD

The following morning, on his way to the office, Zack received a text from Suzy asking for a meeting with him, Will Thomason, and Ben Lehman. She wondered if he could set up the meeting in New York City.

The text caught Zack off guard. "What does Ben Lehman want?" He decided to wait to answer Suzy's text until he got to his office building. *I'll discuss this with Frederick*, he thought as he entered Grey's office. Zack explained the text from Suzy and waited for an answer. Instead of replying to Zack, Grey picked up the phone and called Karl Strass in New York. They spoke for a few minutes. Then Frederick told Zack that the meeting would be set up at their New York office on

Fifth Avenue. Dinner would be arranged for the three of them. This would afford them more privacy. (The office was bugged.) Zack agreed. He would find out Will's schedule and then set the time with Suzy, who would relay it to Ben Lehman.

Zack had to figure out how to present Ben Lehman to Will Thomason. Why would I set up a meeting with an Israeli just months before the election?

Secretly breaking Will away from the campaign was not an easy task. Not telling Christie was even harder. "It will be a relaxing break from campaigning. We are going to meet with some old college buddies in New York City for a few hours and be back late the same night," Zack explained.

The night of the meeting, Will and Zack's plane landed at Teterboro Airport in New Jersey by eight o'clock. It was a smaller executive airport away from the maddening crowd. It took about one and a half hours to get to Sixty-Fifth Street and Fifth Avenue in the city.

They took the elevator to the top floor. "My firm owns this floor," Zack explained. When they entered, the caterer was setting up. A beautiful Asian woman was in charge, and the food looked and smelled great. Ben was waiting, with a drink in hand, looking out at the city lights. They all shook hands and sat down around the conference table.

"Senator Thomason, my name is Ben Lehman. I am an investigator for the Israeli Knesset. They have asked me to set up this meeting to meet and get to know you. If or when you become president, what will be your administration's policy toward Israel? You mentioned foreign aid in your last speech. As you know, we receive three billion a year from the United States, and we are your friends." Will agreed that Israel was a close ally and listened to what else Ben had to say.

The food was very good. Will drank water. They discussed several different subjects. Ben brought up the fact that the Palestinians still refuse to discuss peace and Hamas is still launching missiles into Israel. Will sometimes looked over at Zack with a questioning look but said nothing.

Ben finally got to the topic of Iran. He wanted to know what Will thought of their nuclear program.

Will was careful in his reply but felt the program had to end. "My policy is that there will be no nukes in the Middle East." That was a big relief to Ben.

It was getting close to eleven o'clock, and Will had to get back to DC. It was an informal evening. They all shook hands and agreed to meet again.

On the drive back to the airport, Will said, "Okay, Zack, what the hell was that all about?"

"Ben Lehman is an old friend, and our firm does a lot of business with his family."

"Who does he work for, the Mossad?" asked Will.

"Why would you think that?"

"In the marines, I spent two years at our mission in Tel Aviv. I met a lot of the support team to the Knesset. He was not one of them. These investigators are good, and they have been there for years. He is too young. What does the Mossad want, and why did you bring me here?"

"Okay, he does work for the Mossad. They are worried about Iran," Zack said. "Our current president will let them go under in a heartbeat. Setting up a meeting with you may have slowed down an attack. At least, I hope so. So I thought it was worth it. I'm sorry, Will. Don't be mad at me. We are so close to war in the Middle East that it's not even funny. Anything we can do to prevent a war must be done."

"How are you involved in these policies? I thought you were just a lawyer, not a diplomat."

"I am just a lawyer, but I also happen to be the best friend of the next president of the United States. So my firm asked me to try to put this meeting together. It was very important to the Israelis. And Will, don't tell Christie." The look Zack got back wasn't pretty.

CHAPTER 49

THE RALLY

The July 5 rally was only two days away. Will's team felt that if thirty to forty thousand people attended, they were really doing well.

When Will was fifteen, his mom and dad had taken him to New York City for New Year's Eve to watch the ball drop in Times Square. They'd wanted him to experience the excitement of the moment. Well, it had been exciting. There'd been more people in one place than he had ever seen before.

When Will walked out on the stage at the National Mall, he was stunned. New Year's Eve was nothing compared to this. The Mall was full. There had to be more than one hundred thousand people in attendance. Who knew? The noise was deafening. He just stood there in awe. The crowd would not stop cheering, "WILL WILL GET IT DONE! WILL WILL GET IT DONE!"

Christie stood in the wings with tears in her eyes. It appeared she was going to have to share him with three-hundred million Americans.

The noise ebbed, and Will stepped forward. He looked at all the people silently. Then he spoke. His prepared speech was in front of him, but it didn't fit now. "I can't believe you all came to this little rally." Laughter and cheers rang out. "I am overwhelmed by seeing all of you, and my heart is exploding. I had a speech for today; I forgot it. You have made me tongue-tied." This brought more laughter from the crowd. "You know, I am a tough marine, but who says tough marines don't cry? You have brought tears to my eyes. The fact that you all showed up today and believe in me will make me work harder than ever for you."

"Electing a president is like hiring a CEO for a very large company. When you put your money at risk, he'd better succeed, or he gets fired. The same goes here. When you put your faith in one man to change your life, he'd better succeed. The past four years have been rough. Your CEO has not done the job you hired him for. He's let you down. We have had to live with high unemployment, two percent Gross Domestic Product, and nothing but fighting all the time in Congress. Passing bills you don't want, raising taxes you can't afford AND no jobs, no jobs, no jobs. I can't say that enough.

Okay, let's forget the past. It stinks anyway. Let's look to the future. Our national security comes first. The Middle East is a powder keg, ready to explode. We have to keep a closer eye on the terrorist movements and help our allies defend themselves.

"Next, on the home front, if we cut regulations and cut taxes, small businesses will flourish. Let's build the pipelines. We need to move gas and oil across this country. By lowering our heating bills with natural gas, we'll put more money into our pockets to buy more products we build right here.

Revamping the tax codes and fixing education—that's a good start. One has to wonder why this was not done before. It's not rocket science. Maybe the people you hired in the past couldn't read, or spell J-O-B-S. We have all made a lot of mistakes. We're not perfect, but enough is enough. Dump the ones who are in it for themselves and elect the ones who are in it for the people, who, like me, want to go forward and get our greatness back. I promise you—right here, right now—that I will not fail you! You will not have to fire me. We will talk often about our problems and what we can do to fix them. You will be well informed, just like a shareholder of a top-one-hundred company. Give me your vote, and watch what happens. You won't be sorry. God bless you all, and God bless the United States of America."

The cheering was overwhelming. Will could not believe what was happening. He knew the responsibility he had. He also knew he had broad shoulders. He walked back into the wings to find Christie in tears and all his staff wiping their eyes. They attacked him, hugs and handshakes all around. *Wow*, he thought. *I guess that was a "good speech, but now is not the time to rub it in.*

CHAPTER 50

HOME STRETCH

The rally had been a huge success. The turnout had been larger than anyone could have hoped for. Close to one hundred thousand people had showed up to hear Will's speech. That was the start of the momentum Will needed to pull ahead of the current president.

The campaign had started in California and gone from there to Washington, Colorado, Illinois, and Ohio. It had continued south to Missouri and Alabama and settled for three days in Florida. Now it was time for the big push on the West Coast.

"What day is it?" Will asked Christie as they landed in Will's hometown, Orlando.

"I think it's Tuesday," she replied. "Just two weeks until the election."

"I hope I can make it," Will said.

"You'll make it. Let's go, big guy."

What a slave driver, he thought. There was a huge crowd waiting for him as he stepped off the plane. He waved and called out to the crowd, "It's good to be home. I love you all." The crowd cheered, some people holding signs that read, "WILL WILL GET IT DONE!" Getting into his limo, he headed on to his next fundraiser.

"It's not looking good, sir," said Matt Fulton to President Hutton.

"No shit! What do the polls say?"

"He's up by four points, but it's worse for the Senate. The Republicans might sweep all the Senate seats and give them a majority."

"How did we get outspent? This is a thirty-five-year-old senator with two years of experience. Where did he find all this backing? Someone big must be behind him, someone very powerful and smart. I want to know who. He did not do this alone—no way. Check out all the PACs. I want to know where the money is coming from."

"I'm on it, sir," replied Matt.

Matt Fulton was checking into super PACs that had unlimited funding and no contact with the candidate. He was also checking into who started them. *Even if I find out, it won't make any difference with only two weeks left before the election*, he thought. *But I'll dig in to this anyway. Who knows what I'll find.*

With only a week to go before the elections, Matt Fulton brought the information he'd gathered to the president. "Sir, here is the list of the backers of the super PACs that have been doing all the spending for Will Thomason."

The president perused the information and looked up at Matt. "These are the biggest companies in the country. I can't see why they would back a junior senator. I got a lot of their support in my last election. It just doesn't make any sense. Why would they change so fast?"

"I don't know, Sir."

CHAPTER 51

THE ELECTION

Election day was here. "That was the fastest eighteen months ever," Will said to Christie on their way to vote.

"Time flies when you're having fun," she said.

He looked at her. "You thought this was fun?"

"Didn't you?" she asked.

"Yeah, I guess so. Having you with me made all the difference."

"Oh, how nice," Christie said. "You can't live without me, huh?"

"You're right. I can't. Let's go vote. You *are* voting for me, right?"

"That's privileged," Christie laughingly said.

After voting, they headed to their hotel to watch the results. The Ritz-Carlton Georgetown was a beautiful hotel. The Will Thomason for President Campaign had selected it for the final night and the acceptance party.

As of early evening, the polls showed Will in the lead by five points—a lot to unseat an existing president. He was a nervous wreck. He thought he would have some privacy for a while. No chance. Zack Miller was there, along with the entire staff and campaign manager. *Thank God it was a suite. I guess walking around in my boxer shorts is out of the question*; he thought and laughed to himself. He noticed Christie looking at him, probably reading his mind. *Man, she doesn't miss a thing.*

He was tired. He headed to the bedroom, hoping Christie would follow. She did. He lay down on the bed, and she snuggled next to him. Not ten minutes later, they were both asleep. The day, the excitement, and all the hard work had taken its toll on both of them.

What is all that pounding? Will thought as he was awakened from a sound sleep. Christie looked up and then checked her watch. He opened the door, and the crowd flowed in, screaming and laughing and hugging them. It appeared that Will Thomason, the thirty-six-year-old senator from Florida, a US marine, had just been elected as the next president of the United States.

Holy shit, he thought. Christie hugged him and kissed him, and her tears started flowing. He looked at her, and they both started laughing. "We did it," he said. "You were right. We *are* a good team."

He waved his hands to get some order. "I just want to say thank you for all of your hard work. We could never have done this without each and every one of you.

Zack came over and hugged Will and Christy and told them how thrilled he was. "I knew you could do it!"

It was a beautiful, cold day in Washington for this January 20 inauguration. Christie looked stunning in a violet-gray designer coat, as she sat, beaming with pride, at Will as he took his oath of office. The word was already out that this handsome young president, Will Thomason, would be marrying Christie Adams in the White House in June.

Everyone's eyes were on the beautiful couple as they attended the inaugural balls. Will was handsome in his black tuxedo. Christie wore a deep-blue silk gown that complemented her beautiful blue eyes. The form fitting dress had long sleeves and a square neckline that accentuated her fabulous figure. Her jewelry was a diamond drop on a simple silver necklace and diamond loop earrings. It was at the first ball that they announced their upcoming nuptials.

In New York City, on the sixty-fifth floor, seven men were watching the inauguration on TV. "Well, we have our man in the White House. We should all be very proud of a job well done."

CHAPTER 52

THE BEGINNING

Three months later, the new president had gotten through his first few months in office and was settling in to his job. There was so much to accomplish: first, national security. He started to look into the Middle East. Iran was still going nuclear. Israel wanted to move forward with talks with the president. Of course, bolstering the economy and creating jobs were also some of his top priorities. He put his team to work. They had to clean up the mess the last administration had left for them. With the help of both houses, he was hoping it was going to be done quickly.

As president, there wasn't enough time in the day. He spent half his time interviewing candidates for his new cabinet positions and the other half in meetings. He still hadn't had time to sit down with the congressional leaders. He realized that instituting the laws was a lot more complicated than writing them.

The wedding plans were in full swing for a June ceremony. The whole world was waiting with anticipation for the first White House wedding in fifty years. Everyone wanted to see the young leader of the free world marry his beautiful bride.

EPILOGUE

It was a cold and clear night in New York City. The quarterly meeting of the Solution Committee was coming to order. The new chairman was just coming into view on the closed-circuit television. "Good evening, gentlemen," he said.

"Good evening, Mister President."

Coming soon Book II
Solution Committee Looks at the World

AUTHOR BIO

New York native Jon Grimm lives with his family in central Florida. A retired businessman, Grimm is a political junkie and avid reader of thrillers. He finally has time to not only read but also write his own stories. *Solution Committee* is his first novel.